DYZTURBIA

Should Have Stayed Home

Copyright

Copyright © 2016, Dyzturbya – Should Have Stayed Home by Carla Kovach, Brooke Venables, Vanessa Morgan, Mark Wallace, John Lovell.

Disclaimer

All characters appearing in this work are fictitious. Any resemblance to real persons, living or dead, is purely coincidental.

Contents

Ludicro by Carla Kovach

The Curse of Cassia by Vanessa Morgan

Agathe by Brooke Venables

The Cliff House by Mark Wallace

Return of the Ripper by John Lovell

Ludicro
By
Carla Kovach

I am a lie,
But you see truth.
I need your soul,
But you'll not gift.
I'm your desire,
But you'll not see.
I'm ludicrous,
For your soul, I'm he.

*****

Lydia leaned back in her seat, eyes closed, with one hand on her head whilst intricately weaving a strand of hair around her index finger. The coach went over a bump in the road, then the toddler kicked the back of her seat, again. The driver braked and pipped his horn, forcing everyone to thrust forward. She swallowed, forcing the nausea back, then she pulled the hair out at the root and dropped the black strand to the floor. She wiped her sweaty brow and looked back, catching a glimpse of the child. The sweaty, red-faced menace began to wail. "It's just down the road Jake, stop playing up. The lady in front will tell you off and you won't like that," the mother shouted. That was the first time the woman had spoken and the brat had been kicking her seat since they had left Dalaman Airport. Little Jake responded by climbing over his mother and running up and down the aisle. The coach started to move again.

"That looks like a mini piece of The Colosseum and look at the fountains. I can't wait to get out of this sweat box and explore," Imogen said. The small village square looked busy. People were reading papers while sitting in cafes eating lunch. A group of children pointed at the dolphin statues in the fountains. Lydia stared out of the window as she was about to extract another hair. Imogen gently took her hand and guided it back to her lap.

"Why did I agree to come away with you?"

Imogen slipped down her sunglasses and peered over them. "Because it's been a long time and you've missed me," Imogen replied.

"There is that."

Screaming boy yelled again as his mother dragged him out of the coach aisle and forced him back into his seat whereupon he continued kicking and screaming. They pulled up outside The Chateau, their hotel for the holiday. Its beautiful boutique image sported a small turret on the top of the building. Behind it, tree covered mountains reached heights she couldn't fathom. Out the front were some tables and chairs that were set for dinner. She looked through the gap in the people sitting to her left and momentarily had a clear view of the sea. She pictured herself sitting at those tables, enjoying a meal while gazing out at the sea, taking time to reflect on her life, losing Oscar, and her newly resumed friendship with Imogen. Never again would she allow family to come between them. It had been too long and her life hadn't been the same when they'd gone their separate ways. Imogen had forgiven her and now it was time to start afresh.

"I think this week is going to be one to remember. Welcome to Içmeler," Imogen said as she stood and threw her bag over her shoulder. "Come on lazy, get up. We have a holiday to enjoy and it starts now." Lydia looked back and noticed that the mother and screaming boy were still seated. At least they weren't staying in the same hotel. She followed Imogen off the coach.

They waited at reception and a man in his mid-twenties welcomed them in. Lydia removed the booking details from her bag and passed them to him. "I see, you want a room on the top floor, with a sea view. We have keeping just the room for you," he said in broken

English with a smile. "I am Firat. Anything you need, just ask." He took Lydia's case, placed it on a trolley and walked towards the lift.

"What about Imogen's case?" Lydia asked, staring at the man. The man stared back, smiled and continued into the lift. "Wait, my friend-"

"It's okay Lyd, he doesn't understand. I'll get my own." Imogen wheeled her case into the lift.

They reached their floor. Firat walked ahead with the trolley. "I can't believe he didn't take your case. I'm going to say something."

Imogen yanked Lydia's arm and pulled her back. "Lydia no. It's our first day. We don't want to make a scene." Firat looked back as he opened the door to their room. Lydia released herself from Imogen's grip and walked ahead into the room.

"Are you okay Madam?" Lydia ignored him. Her eyes were drawn to the view through the patio doors. The blue tones of the sea blended in with the sky, making the horizon invisible. Mountains jutted out from the sea, and the bay of Marmaris could be seen in the distance. The man continued to stand.

"I think he wants a tip," Imogen whispered.

"I'm not giving him anything," Lydia replied as she ignored him. He eventually left. "What a cheek. He really thought he was getting a tip after the way he treated you. I don't believe it, and to top it off we've got a double bed. I asked for twin beds." She began pacing the floor and biting her nails. "I'm going to have to say something."

"Don't. It doesn't matter. It'll be like when we were kids and I stayed at yours. Really, it doesn't matter. Let's just enjoy our holiday," Imogen replied.

Lydia walked over to the patio doors and slid them open. As she stepped onto the balcony she felt a faint breeze cutting through the wall of heat. "You're right. I'm going to put my feet up for a bit, check out the minibar and then unpack."

"I'm going to explore the village a bit. Want to come?" Imogen asked.

"No. I'm exhausted. I'm just going to stay here and chill."

Moments later, Lydia watched from the balcony as Imogen walked towards the fountains that they'd passed on the coach. She looked up and waved. Lydia waved back. Soon her friend had disappeared into the distance.

Lydia walked across the room to her bag, took out her camera and lenses, and placed them on the patio table on the balcony. She needed to get back to reality after the shock of losing Oscar. Her mother's words rang through her head. "Well, he did ride a motorbike. I can't believe you got on it with him after I told you how I felt. He'll kill you one day. Thank goodness you weren't with him that day, stupid boy. It was only a matter of time." The woman had failed to realise that Oscar was a safe rider. It wasn't his fault. He always made sure she'd worn leathers and a helmet, and he never even sped on the bike. No, the cow hadn't realised that as she'd tried her hardest to tarnish his memory.

A tear rolled down her cheek as she remembered her long haired chef and his wide smile that had made her so happy. She wiped a trail of wet from her arm and held it up, blood. There was no way she was ever going to be able to stop picking at her arms. The scab fell off, leaving a tiny but angry red hole, in and around the blood pool. She wiped it away.

Taking her hair, she began to twist the underlayer around her finger until she pulled a few strands out. Her fingertip gently brushed her nape and felt the prickles of new strands poking out of the bald patch under her hair. "Stop it," she heard her mother yell. That's all her mother ever had to say. "Stop it, you'll go bald, take up knitting or something." Her mother just didn't understand. Imogen understood, she always did. She picked up the camera and exchanged the standard lens for a telephoto lens and looked through it. From behind the camera she observed the beach below.

A couple of teenagers were playing a game that involved throwing each other in the sea. She smiled as she watched them. The girl in the blue bikini was being carried in a fireman's lift by a hefty looking boy. He waded through the water, carrying the screaming girl until he was at waist height, then he threw her into the sea. She immediately came back up to the surface and began splashing him while laughing. Lydia's focus went back to the beach and she watched a waiter carrying a tray of drinks over to a sun lounger. Every image that she focused on wasn't worthy of snapping. Her inspiration had dried up. She leaned back on the patio chair and refocused on the tall man standing at the water's edge. Shaking, she zoomed in closer. His long brown hair fell over his shoulders. "Oscar," she whispered. The man turned. She trembled as another tear rolled down her cheek.

"Don't be stupid. He's gone," her mother's voice shouted in her head. She was right. He had the build, he had the hair, but he wasn't Oscar.

A woman ran up to him and kissed him on the lips. Lydia looked away and wiped her teary eyes. She glanced back. Oscar's gaze met hers through the camera. He let go of the woman and continued staring. Tears of blood began dripping down his face as he reached up to her. She pulled the camera away and rubbed her aching eyes before looking back. The man was still kissing the woman. "Stupid, stupid," she said as she placed the camera down on the table and put her feet up on another chair. She grabbed her sunglasses and leaned her head against the patio doors. "Too much sun and no sleep last night," she whispered as she took a deep breath and closed her eyes.

*****

Cold, why was she so cold? She took one step after another but she wasn't getting any closer. "Babe, I'm here," Oscar called. She gazed up at him, his head was perfectly framed by the moon, giving him a milky halo. She reached around her neck for her camera but she didn't have it. Great, she'd tried hard to get the perfect photo for so long, now was her chance, but she didn't have her camera. His smile beamed back at her. She ran, longing for his embrace, his warmth. She tripped and shivered. Why was she so cold when Oscar was wearing nothing but swimming shorts while standing at the sea's edge? Like a pond, the sea was still. Oscar took another step into the water. "It's beautiful. Kick your shoes off and come in."

"I'll get my clothes wet," she said as she pushed each foot forward though the pebbly beach until she reached him. "How did you get here?"

"I've been waiting for you. I knew you'd come."

She held her breath and stroked his face. An image of him in hospital, hooked up to a life support machine, shot through her thoughts. "You're not real."

"You're touching me." He leaned in and kissed her hard on the lips. "I've missed you so much." Tears flooded her face. She gasped between cries as she gripped him hard, taking in his smell and running her hands through his knotty hair.

"I've missed you so much too. I thought you … you-" she pulled away and stared at his unshaven face.

He smiled and took her hand, placing it close to his heart. "You can feel my heart beating. What does that tell you?"

"But-"

"Come swim with me," he said as he waded deeper into the gentle water.

Lydia shook her head. "Don't leave me."

"Come with me."

"I can't, I'm so cold," she replied through chattering teeth. Oscar dived underneath the water's surface. "Oscar," she called. He didn't reappear. "Oscar. Stop playing games." He bobbed back up and beckoned her to enter. She kicked off her shoes and stepped into the sea. Oscar swam further out and called her. She shook her head and shivered. "It's too cold. Come back." She watched as he ignored her calls and swam away. He reached the safety rope and lifted it up. "Oscar, please come back." Her heart raced as she hugged herself to keep warm.

      She heard a rumble in the distance. The water's edge receded, revealing a seabed of shale, stones, weed and sand. Oscar was gone. The glint of the moon bounced off his shoulders as he swam away. Another rumble filled the air followed by a whooshing, like a tornado gathering momentum around her head. "Oscar," she yelled as she took a step back. She could no longer see him. Her heart hammered and she began to hyperventilate as she saw the enormous wall of water coming over the mountain that jutted out of the sea. Holding her ears, she ran backwards, screaming and trembling as the approaching tsunami blocked the moon's light and whooshed forward. There was no way she could outrun a wall of water that was the height of a tower block. She kneeled before it, begging it to take her. She could go with Oscar into the sea and they could be together once again. "I'm coming Oscar," she yelled as she sobbed into her gritty hands.

      "Miss. Are you okay?" asked a large man, who was walking with a woman. Lydia looked around. How had she got onto the beach? She remembered falling asleep on the balcony. A tsunami flashed through her mind. She trembled. "Are you okay?" the woman asked.

"What?" She wiped the sweat off her nose and lifted her tee-shirt away from her clammy skin.

"Do you need a doctor?"

"I'm okay. Where's the tsunami?"

The man turned and whispered to the woman. She heard the word drugs in their conversation. As she stood, she brushed the pebbles embedded in her knees onto the ground and turned to walk back to the hotel. "Drugs," she said as she shook her head and crossed the road by the mini supermarket.

As she entered the hotel, Firat ran over to her. "Are you okay?"

She grabbed a flyer off the front desk and began fanning her face. "Why wouldn't I be?" As she went to speak again, she caught her reflection in a mirror behind the reception desk. Dried blood streaked her arm. Her hair was all matted and stuck around her face revealing her bald area, her knees were raw from kneeling on the beach, and she didn't have her shoes on. A flashback to her kicking them off as she stepped into the sea came back to her.

"Okay. If you need any assistance, just call down from your room."

She continued into the lift and to her room. Maybe Imogen had returned. She entered the dark room and called her friend's name but there was no reply. Maybe she had returned, found the place empty so went back out. Lydia peeled her sticky clothes off and dropped them to the floor then climbed into bed. Tomorrow was another day. She curled up on her side, in the dark, under the crisp sheet and thought of her moment on the beach. The whole episode, dream or whatever it was, slowly came back to her and she sobbed. Being so close to Oscar had felt real, so real she had smelt him and felt the warmness of his breath on her face. She had lost him all over again. She brought her knees up and cried into the pillow, hugging it until she fell asleep.

*****

Lydia had awoken early and left Imogen sleeping. She hadn't heard her return in the night. As she walked along the seafront towards the marina, she passed a lovely restaurant, serving people breakfast on a small jetty. She smiled as she watched a girl throwing bread in the sea and shouting at her parents, telling them that the fish were eating it. As she neared a bend in the path she reached an ornate water fountain. She placed her camera down and splashed a bit of cold water onto her face before continuing up the steeper hill, away from the marina. Everyone would be snapping away at the boats, she needed something more unusual, a different perspective, so she headed up the hill and followed the road.

    She lifted her camera and looked through the lens. That was what she was after, a rusting old mesh with the beauty of the bay captured in every gap. As she continued walking it became quieter. She heard a bell ringing in the distance. Moments later she reached what she had come to see, the derelict hotel. Shrubs and bushes had partially taken over the crumbling steps that led to the main building and apartments. Pushing the branches aside, she climbed the steps, one by one, until she reached the top. She grabbed her camera and snapped away. A clunky bell sound came from the hills. She squinted in the direction of the noise, and what sounded like a crying child pierced her thoughts. "Hello," she called. The sound was met by the wailing of many. She crept towards the main building and called again. There was no reply. The wailing subsided. "Don't lose it Lydia," she said. She shook her head and continued walking.

  Standing in front of the chipped white building, she began taking more photos. She needed to explore properly, set up a few shots. She stepped through the door frame and took one step into the empty stone hallway and listened for any sign of life. A rustling drew her eyes to the room on the left. Her heart began to pound. She held her camera up towards the room and took a silent snap. A loud shriek echoed through the building. She stepped back and tripped over a piece of debris. Shuffling backwards on her bottom, she crouched under a flight of stairs and waited, hoping that whatever was making the noise would leave the building. She lifted her camera up and flicked to the last photo she'd taken. She exhaled and laughed as she saw a photo of a small bird entangled in an old bit of mattress that was stuck to a piece of bed frame.

  She smiled as she released the bird's wing allowing it to fly out of the window. Ambling around the rest of the building, she took more photos. Upstairs were more rooms and balconies. Rubble, broken sinks, toilets and door frames, all covered the floors. She stopped at the top of the building and stared at the sea through the torn window mesh. A jet ski skimmed the water and trip boats left the marina for the day. With other buildings to explore, she left.

    From what she'd read, there was still a long building and some sort of pump room to find. She headed through a stone arch and up some more steps to reach the long building. She peered in one of the rooms and sniggered at the graffiti picture of a vagina that greeted her. Her heart beat faster as she photographed the decay, the debris and the beer bottles; evidence of current human activity and evidence that her inspiration was returning. Her smile vanished as her ears tuned in again to the child-like wailing that filled the air. The wailing was followed by a rumbling of hooves. "Go away," she yelled as she ran out of the building.

    Clunking bells were all around her along with the goats that they were attached to. The brown and white horned goat stopped wailing and stood in front of her, staring directly at her with its devilish rectangular pupils. The other goats stopped. They remained still and silent behind their leader. The sound of birds, jet skis and boats stopped. It was her and the silent goats. Her heart hammered as she took a slight step back. She felt a trail of sweat dripping down her neck, tickling her skin. She wanted to scratch, she needed to wipe it away. The goat bleated as it leaned down to chew a flower. The others joined in and began to bleat and wail like babies. She stepped back and kicked a stone which chipped the wall of the building. The horned goat scarpered, followed by the rest. She exhaled and smiled as they ran away. It was goats, just goats. She began the trek uphill towards the pump room where she wanted to take a few more photos before heading back to meet Imogen.

*****

Imogen was up, dressed and sitting on the balcony when she returned to the hotel. "I did pop back to see if you wanted to come out last night but you were gone with the fairies when I checked on you."

Lydia placed her camera on the side and joined her friend. "Sorry. I wasn't much fun was I?"

"I get it. You needed to catch up with your sleep. We're here to relax and do as little or as much as you want. Anyway, I got talking to a few people in a café in the main square and went with them to a bar. It was really good, honestly. They're going to be there tonight if you fancy joining them for a drink, with me I mean." Lydia stared at the beach, ignoring her friend. The man who she'd mistaken for Oscar was there again with his girlfriend. "Hello, anyone there Lydia?" Lydia leaned forward and squinted to get a better look at the man. "There's definitely a resemblance," Imogen said.

Lydia wiped a tear from her cheek. "I miss him. I was so sure it was him." Imogen placed her arms around her friend and stroked her hair. "What would I do without you?"

"Look. I'm going to pop out and do a bit of shopping. Have you seen the bags? They're to die for. Are you coming?"

"No. Sorry, I know I should make an effort but I just can't, not yet." Lydia began picking at her arm.

"Okay, but don't wallow all day and leave your arm alone. Go downstairs to the bar or something. Oscar wouldn't want you to give up." Lydia rolled her eyes and continued to stare at the beach.

"I haven't given up. I just need time to settle, besides, it's too hot for me to walk around and look at bags. You go, have a good time and grab yourself a bargain."

Imogen hugged her friend, smiled and headed to the door. "I'll catch you later. Oh, and one last thing, you're definitely coming out for something to eat with me tonight. No excuses. I haven't seen you eat a thing since we arrived. Make sure you're ready for seven."

"Yes Sir," Lydia called as Imogen left.

She grabbed her camera off the side and began perusing the photos she'd taken earlier. The contrast of the pink flowers against the decaying building were truly stunning. As soon as she arrived home, she would get to work editing the collection before marketing them to the various travel magazines she'd sold to in the past. She flinched as she reached a photo of the lead goat staring down the lens. Somehow she'd managed to capture a close-up of its eye. She swallowed then flicked to the next lot of images. She remembered the pump room with its steep steps. The inside of the small sugar cube building had a thin walkway with a plunge into darkness either side. Ladders led the way into the bowels of the darkness but she hadn't been brave enough to continue. Instead she'd used her flash and taken a few pot luck shots of what the darkness might be hiding. She flicked forward and all she could see were pipes, ladders and decaying walls until Oscar filled her screen. His naked torso was flecked with dirt. His normally soft hair was stuck in matted clumps to his shoulder and the look in his blood shot eyes begged her to help him. She wept as she traced his face with her fingertip. "I didn't know you were there," she said as she wept.

"I need you," he replied as his cries became distorted. "We need to be together."

"Go away," she yelled as she looked away. "You're not real. Leave me alone." She picked up the camera and stared at the photo. He had done as she'd asked and left her alone. She gasped and fell to her knees in front of the camera. "I'm sorry, I didn't mean it. Please … come back …. Come back."

"Miss. Are you okay? You need doctor?" asked the old woman holding the cloth.

The moment was broken by the pungent smell of disinfectant. Lydia stared at the cleaning cloth dangling in front of her.

"I did knock Miss but there no answer. I hear you call and think, accident. I clean see," she said as she held up the cloth.

"I'm so sorry. I'm okay. I don't need a doctor but thank you," Lydia replied, her cheeks burning. She caught a glimpse of her arm and noticed a trail of blood. She'd been picking her scabs again. She looked away. Why did she have to pick again, especially for everyone else to see?

"I get some plaster," the woman said as she left the room.

Lydia looked at the photo one last time, confirming that Oscar wasn't there. The cleaner re-entered with a first aid box. She knew she had to get out and make some connections with the real world. Imogen was right, she was going out tonight. She was going out to spend time with real people. Oscar was gone. She had to make an effort to re-enter reality.

*****

"Oh my God. You look stunning," Imogen said as she greeted Lydia on the balcony and handed her a beer from the mini bar. "That black dress, when I saw it in the shop, I just knew it had you written all over it. I'm not sure about the pumps though but you know best."

"I love these pumps." Lydia sipped the beer from the bottle and blushed. She looked at her watch, it was almost seven. "I'm starving. Shall we go?" she asked as she placed the rest of the beer back in the fridge.

"Ready as a ready thing. I'm glad you've found your appetite. I'm thinking steak. What say you?"

"Steak sounds good," Lydia replied as they left the room.

As they passed reception, Firat smiled and waved. "Good night to you."

The warmth of the early evening smacked her as she left the air conditioned reception. Imogen linked her arm in Lydia's as they continued to walk down the steps onto the uneven path. The sounds of a chilled-out duet came from the large hotel on the beachfront.

They strolled together along the promenade, over the canal bridge and past a seafront café which was showing off a huge strawberry tart in a glass display cabinet. Her mouth watered. She tried to think back to the last time she'd eaten a proper meal. It was a day after Oscar's accident. Her mother had bought her a bag of chips from their local takeaway. She'd eaten a few but they'd jarred in her throat every time she'd tried to swallow. She remembered her mother coming up to see what she'd eaten and insisting on another chip. That chip had lodged in her throat, forcing her to heave it back up into her bin, after a moment of panic. Ever since, she'd taken the food thing slowly and just sucked on boiled sweets, or melted chocolate in her mouth. It was only now, after passing the strawberry tart that she felt her appetite really coming back. They took a left turn away from the sea and followed the path until they reached the main square. Imogen led her to The Lighthouse Restaurant. They were greeted by a waiter and seated near the front, and given a menu.

"What are you having? Is it two steaks?" Imogen asked.

Lydia leaned back in her chair and caught a glimpse of the dessert display. "Strawberry cake, I think. I don't fancy a steak or anything heavy."

"You need a proper meal Lydia. Please have a meal." Imogen looked down and brushed her hand through her hair.

The last thing Lydia wished to do was disappoint her friend. Poor Imogen had gone out alone the previous night, she'd shopped alone all day and now all she wanted was for Lydia to enjoy a meal with her. She swallowed and looked up. "You're right. I think I'll try a steak. I might not manage it all though so don't be disappointed in me."

"I'll never be disappointed in you. I'm only thinking of you and you needing to keep your strength up. That's what best friends are for." A tear rolled down Lydia's cheeks. "Don't cry. We're going to get through this together. A bad thing happened, you loved him, I totally understand."

Lydia pulled a tissue from the holder on the table. "It's not that. I can't believe you still want to be my friend after everything. You were the best person in my life back then. You know what my mum was like, I don't know why she had it in for you."

"I suppose she just had your interests at heart. Don't hate her for it. We're together now, that's all that matters."

A waiter approached the table and smiled. "What would you like to drink?" He paused and stared as he spoke. "Oh it's you. The dress looks very nice. Right choice." Lydia looked at Imogen.

"I showed his friend who works in one of the shops a photo of you when I was choosing your dress earlier. We had to guess your size. Sorry," Imogen said with a smile.

Lydia smiled. "Thank you, definitely the right choice. Right, make it a bottle of white and two fillet steaks, and a piece of that strawberry cake."

"Okay. Whatever you want, coming up," the waiter replied as he glanced back at the man who was pouring drinks behind the bar.

A good while passed as the friends chatted and laughed. The food then arrived. The waiter placed one steak in front of Lydia and the other one in the middle of the table. He smiled and turned as he was called away by another customer. "Charming, he could've finished serving us before dashing off," Lydia said as she lifted the plate in the middle of the table and placed it in front of Imogen. She lifted up her glass and smiled. "Anyway, let's toast to a brilliant holiday and brilliant memories."

She ate a few chips then gave the steak a prod with her fork. She chewed and chewed but she couldn't swallow the mass that was filling her mouth. She felt a familiar tickle at the back of her throat. She needed to cough. She needed to eject the food and quick. She coughed the food into a serviette and gasped for breath.

"Can I get you anything? Water?" the waiter asked as he ran over. She turned and was confronted by Oscar.

She felt her face burning up as she gasped for air. She looked away. "It's not real, it's not real," she whispered. Her hands began to tingle. She dragged her trembling fingers through her sweaty hair and yanked it down. Looking out towards the square, she stared at the dolphin fountain ahead, focusing on it, trying to distract her thoughts away from Oscar but the street swayed back and forth. She turned and looked again. Everyone was staring at her and everyone was Oscar, except for Imogen.

"Come with me," the Oscar chorus called. "I love you, come with me."

"Lydia, what's up?" Imogen asked.

"He's here. He's everywhere. I have to go. Can you sort the bill out? I'll pay you back later," Before Imogen had the chance to reply, Lydia stood and ran out of the restaurant, back towards the beach. She turned. Oscar was gone. A sea of faces stared and pointed as she staggered along the uneven path. The waiter kept shouting something, then he ditched a tray of drinks and walked towards her.

"Get back. Stop," he called as he picked up his pace.

She ran until she reached the seafront, then she crouched behind the bushes that separated the promenade and the beach, and held her breath. The waiter passed her and stopped before turning back. Why had he chased her? As she heard his footsteps run off in the distance she gasped for breath and coughed. "What's happening to me?" she said as she wiped the tears from her face. A small black cat brushed past her hip, meowing for attention. She fell onto the sand and pulled her knees up towards her chin and rocked back and forth. The cat continued to nudge her hip until she reached out and stroked it. She laid her legs out flat, in the dark, on the beach, and allowed the cat to sit on her lap. "What's wrong with me cat?" Tears fell down her chin. As the cat brushed against her, a few strands of its fur stuck to her tears.

"I keep telling you I love you. There's nothing wrong. I need you Lyddy. It was always you and me," the cat said in Oscar's voice. She stood, ejecting the cat off her lap. The cat meowed and scarpered.

"Go away," she yelled as she ran along the promenade back towards the hotel. People stared as she stumbled around, telling Oscar's voice to leave her alone. She passed Firat in reception and waited for the lift. She felt his gaze on her back bearing down like a ton weight. "Why are you taking so long?" she asked as she pressed the call button over and over again.

"Are you okay?" Firat asked. She looked up. Behind him, the normally well-lit reception seemed to have a dark presence about it. A shadow crawled across the wall and expanded until the whole wall was dark grey. She shivered as the grey passed her face. "Miss," he said. She ran up the stairs, grabbing the cool metal rail as she fled. As she reached the room she burst through the door, jumped into bed and dragged a sheet over her body and head, blocking the room and the world, out. Placing her fingers in her ears and rocking back and forth, she vowed that the next day would be a better one. She only hoped that Imogen would forgive her for running away from the restaurant. She closed her eyes and tried to dream of better times. Oscar was in her dream but he wasn't scaring her. Things were like before. They were in his bedsit smoking weed and listening to the Foo Fighters, Oscar's favourite band. They'd spent their last weekend making love, eating and drinking in bed all day before his shift, planning their lives together and looking for a flat. She wanted to be back there, lost in that moment with Oscar. She sobbed as she allowed sleep to take over.

*****

Shivering, she opened her eyes. Why was she on the beach? The sea was calm and she couldn't hear a soul anywhere. It was still dark but she imagined it was probably nearly morning. She wrapped her arms around her body. Her heart raced when she felt her flesh and realised that she was standing on the beach in her bra and pants.

"I can't believe you still do this. I remember the first time you walked in the night, scared the life out of me. The doctors told me you'd grow out of this sleepwalking malarkey," she remembered her mum once saying. Looking around, she realised she was alone. She heard a rowdy group of men shouting in the distance. Her focus turned to her hotel room. There was a lamp on. A figure walked in front of the window. She shivered as another figure joined it before they disappeared past her line of sight. The rowdy group of men were getting nearer. She ran back towards the hotel, not wanting a scene.

"Whoa, look who's had too much of a good night out," one of the men shouted. The others laughed. One man tripped on the curb and fell into the gutter. She heard another one of the group vomiting, then the rest jeered.

She ran and didn't stop until she reached their room. The room was now in darkness. "Imogen?" She crept forward not wanting to walk in on her friend and the man she may've picked up. "I'm coming in Imogen." She passed the bed. A beam of moonlight lit up the outlines of two bodies lying in the bed. She pulled the curtain open a little more so that she could open the patio door. Maybe, just maybe she could sleep on the balcony.

The bodies stirred. "You came back," Oscar's voice said. Imogen lay asleep next to him, gently purring as she breathed in and out. Naked, he stepped out of the bed and walked over to her. He reached out for her and placed his arms around her back and unclipped her bra.

"You're not real-"

"Shhh. You'll wake Imogen up." He placed his finger gently over her mouth and caressed her cheek. She closed her eyes as he kissed her neck, eventually meeting her lips. Sliding the patio open, he nudged her onto the balcony. With every stroke and touch she felt the small hairs on her arms and neck stand. He pressed against her, pushing her against the wall. She grabbed his hair, kissed him and sunk her fingers into his back just like the last time they were together in his bedsit. She wanted it again, she wanted to roll around in the sheets and feel him in her and on her and being part of her. She needed to be at one with him, to feel his breath on her neck.

"Lydia. Is that you?" Imogen called. Oscar stopped and held his finger to his mouth. She didn't make a sound. He placed his mouth over hers while looking into her eyes. She stroked his hair. "Lydia?"

She parted from his kiss. "I'll come in soon. Just getting some fresh air." She turned back and smiled at Oscar but he'd gone. "Oscar? No. Come back."

Imogen appeared by the door with their bed sheet wrapped around her body. Lydia stood there, bra in one hand, head in the other. "You owe me a whole thirty-five lira," Imogen said with her eyes half shut. "Fancy ditching me like that."

"What was Oscar doing here when I got back?"

"Do you know how absurd that sounds? Come on, let me help you into bed." Imogen gently took Lydia's arm, led her to their bed and helped her in.

"I'm not an invalid," she said as she snatched the sheet off Imogen and pulled it over her bare breasts.

"I never said you were. I was just trying to help," Imogen replied as she got into bed and dragged a bit of the blanket back over her side. "Now let's get some sleep. Night-night Lyd."

"Night-night Imogen." She lay there and listened to the sounds of the night through the open balcony door. The group of men had long passed and all was silent. She listened to the gentle lapping of the sea. The lapping turned into a silence that moments later turned into a roar. "I'm scared I'll drown. What if the tsunami gets us?"

"There are no tsunamis in Içmeler," Imogen whispered as she turned over and placed a loving arm around Lydia and kissed her on the cheek. "I'll look after you, now go to sleep.

"I love you Imogen. Best friends forever. Remember?"

"I remember. Besties forever."

Lydia held her friend's hand in the dark and closed her eyes until she drifted off. There were no tsunamis in Içmeler. Imogen always knew best.

*****

She stirred then grabbed her watch from the bedside table. Eleven, it was almost lunch-time.

There was a note on the bed.

I'm downstairs having breakfast. Come join me when you wake Sleepy Head and hurry because I'm bored. Imogen. XX

Lydia smiled and placed the note down. The warmth beat in through the glass door. She walked over and looked at the beach and the calm sea, and smiled. Today was the day she would start again and get out a bit more, visit some cafés, go shopping and take some more photos. After washing and dressing, she skipped down the stairs and passed reception.

"Morning Miss," Firat called.

"Lovely morning it certainly is," she replied. He smiled as she passed.

Imogen was sitting at the table nearest to the road. She turned and waved. Two people were eating breakfast with their children at the next table. The youngest boy dropped his ball and it rolled towards Lydia. She bent and picked it up. "There you go," she said as she handed him his ball.

"What do you say Daniel?" his mother said.

"Thank you," he shouted as he ran back to his table.

Lydia smiled before sitting opposite Imogen. "How long have you been up?"

"About two hours. You looked tired so I thought I'd make myself scarce and leave you to sleep in peace." Imogen paused. "I was worried about you last night. You kept waffling on about Oscar and tsunamis and you ditched me in that restaurant. What was all that about?"

A single tear rolled down Lydia's cheek. "I don't know how to say this. I keep seeing him. He's everywhere and I don't know how to make it stop. I think I'm going crazy." Her face reddened and more tears followed.

"You're not crazy, you're grieving. It's probably because of the man on the beach, the one who looks like him. I mean, that would be enough to make me crazy."

"It's not that. He's everywhere. The cat …. Even a cat on the beach spoke in his voice. What's happening to me?" Lydia held her hand and realised that she'd pulled a clump of hair out. Dropping it to the floor, she turned to Imogen. "Look what this is doing to me," she yelled as she held out her scabby arms. Her tears dripped onto the ground. The couple eating breakfast placed their cutlery down and called their two children over.

"Mummy, why is that lady talking to herself?" the boy asked as he gripped his ball.

Lydia gasped and stepped back. Imogen's translucent figure was sitting at the table, fading until she vanished. "Imogen," she yelled. The family walked out of the hotel restaurant onto the streets and up towards the shops, not looking back, leaving most of their breakfast on the table. "Why did you come back only to leave again? Why? My mother was right. I should never have let you back into my life." The past couple of days flashed through her mind, the looks from Firat, the man chasing her from the restaurant, his recognition of her from when she'd bought the dress from his friend earlier that day. She knocked a chair over as she ran back into the hotel, up the stairs and burst into the room. Only her side of the bed was ruffled. She darted into the bathroom, only her toiletry and make-up bags were on the shelf. She opened the wardrobe, there was only one suitcase, hers. It all made sense. She fell to her knees and sobbed as she picked up her phone and pressed speed dial.

"Mum, it's me."

"Lydia. Where are you? I've been trying to call you for days?"

"I'm on holiday in Turkey, I've had my phone turned off. I told you I needed to get away. I think I'm going mad Mum." She felt her mother's hesitation in responding. "Do you remember Imogen, my friend?"

"I thought we left all that behind fifteen years ago. Remember what the doctor said back then. She's in your mind." Lydia bit the skin around the edge of her nail. "When we lost your dad, it hit us both terribly."

"She's been back Mum. She came here with me and now she's left me. She's gone Mum, she's gone." Lydia wept as she gripped the phone while awaiting her mum's reply.

"Don't cry Love. It's okay. You need to come home. Get the next flight and just come home. We can deal with this together." The woman paused. "It's Oscar's funeral on Friday. I sent some flowers from both of us."

"He's not dead."

"Of course he's dead. Please don't be like this," her mother said.

"You never liked him did you?" she asked as she pulled at her hair.

"That's not true. Let's not do this over the phone. We can talk about this when you get home." Lydia ended the call and threw the phone to the floor and sobbed into her arms. How could he be dead? Yes, there was an accident; yes, he'd been pronounced dead but he was everywhere and in her every thought. She felt his touch, smelt his skin, kissed his lips and enjoyed his warmth. He'd called her, wanted her to go with him and all she'd done was listen to logic. Dead, yes; gone, no. She crawled into bed. She needed to close her eyes and dream of him. If she dreamed, maybe, just maybe, her dream would come true. "I'm ready for you my love," she said as she lay her head on the pillow and stared at the wall. She waited and waited but he did not come. Eventually she closed her eyes and fell asleep.

*****

Imogen entered Lydia's bedroom at home, the one where they'd spent so much time together as children. Maybe they would have a midnight feast or listen to music through her headphones while her mum slept in the room next door. "Have you got the chocolate?" Imogen asked. Lydia reached under her pillow and pulled out a melted bar of milk chocolate. Imogen smiled and opened the wrapper. The melted chocolate stuck to her fingers as she broke it into pieces.

"Watch my sheets, I'll get into trouble," Lydia whispered. Imogen wiped her hand on the crisp white duvet and laughed. She rubbed the chocolate over her face, smudging it in all her facial crevices before wiping the excess on the pillows. "Imogen, stop. Please." She didn't stop. She wiped her hands on the lamp shade, on Lydia's teddies and on the recently ironed pile of clothes that her mum had left out for her to put away.

"Don't be boring Lydia."

Lydia darted across the room and grabbed Imogen's hands as she was about to wipe chocolate on her curtains. "Enough. Get out. I've had enough."

Lydia opened her eyes. She was standing in the dark holding the curtains in the hotel room. Her heart hammered against her ribcage and her mouth was dry. She rubbed her throbbing temples.

"Miss me?" Imogen whispered from behind.

"Go away."

"That's no way to talk to your bestie, your oldest friend, the only person who's ever been there for you," Imogen said.

She turned and saw Imogen's translucent face in front of her. Her eyes didn't blink once, her opaque skin shimmered in waves as a cloud passed the moonlight, allowing the beams back in. "You were never real. I spoke to my mum."

"I spoke to my mum," the apparition said before bursting into uncontrollable bouts of laughter. She felt a shiver run down her spine. "You can feel me, can't you?"

"No, stop it. No," she yelled as she ran back to the bed and jumped in, pulling the sheet over her head. "Go away."

"I will never go away, I love you," the voice said as it changed from Imogen's cackles to Oscar's loving tone.

"Oscar?"

"Don't look at me now. Please, I beg you not to. I'm leaving now but you will find me at the hotel." She went to pull the sheet from her face but an unseen force pulled it gently back over her.

"I'm scared Oscar," she said through chattering teeth. "I'm really scared." She felt his frame straddle her as he stroked her head over the blanket.

"You have nothing to fear. I'll be waiting. The place where you took the photo in the pump room. It was me. I need your help. My soul is trapped and only one person, where the greatest love exists, can free me. We can be together, I promise. I need you and then I will be strong again. We will be strong again."

A billowing wind thrashed through the room blowing the sheet off the bed. Her gaze darted around the room, searching for Oscar. Lydia held her breath and stared in silence. The hotel room was empty, it was dark outside and she was hot, so hot. She wiped her dripping forehead on her pillow and turned the bedside lamp on. She grabbed her camera and flicked back to the photos she took at the abandoned hotel. Oscar had reappeared. Once again, he was in the pump room, awaiting her rescue.

"Help me," he called as the room door flew open. She flung her hand to her pounding heart and stumbled out of bed. He'd called her and opened the door. She knew what she had to do. She straightened her tee-shirt and left the room.

*****

She staggered up the road alongside the marina and reached the abandoned hotel. In darkness she took one step at a time until she reached the main building.

"Help me Lyddy," she heard him call.

Her bare feet were cut and splintered as she passed the main buildings and stepped up the stony pathway that led to the pump room. As she neared the top, the brown and white goat in her photo blocked the way. "Help me Lyddy," the goat said. It stepped towards her and lay down at her feet. She felt its weakness as she stroked its head and passed by, walking until she reached the pump room.

"I'm here Lyddy. Come and get me and we can be together."

The gentle breeze turned into a howling wind as she climbed the steps into the pump room, into the darkness. She shivered as the wind whipped past her ears and around her ankles, sending her slightly off balance. With a steep drop either side she knew she had to stay calm. She swallowed and began to gasp. "Oscar. I'm here."

"I knew you'd come for me." She jumped as the ceiling collapsed on one side of the building, allowing the moon to light up the room. "I'm on the roof, come up."

She looked around. "I can't get up." One of the ladders that led to the depths of the building jutted upwards and led to the roof. She grabbed the nearest rung and climbed until she reached the top. "Oscar," she said as she looked up at her love. His smile, his eyes, and his long hair, were all as she remembered.

He held out his hand and helped her up. "See how beautiful it is here. We have the sea, the lights of Marmaris and we have each other. It's like no one else matters." He leaned in and kissed her gently. "In fact, no one else matters. Did I tell you how much I love you?"

She nodded. "I always knew how much you loved me," she said as she wept and smiled.

"Love you. I'm here now." He grabbed her hand and held it to his heart. She closed her eyes and felt every beat. As time slowed down, she remembered all the fun they'd had. Riding on his bike, their dreams of a big future together, all the meals he'd made her while he'd been doing his chef's training and all the secrets that she'd told him and no one else.

"Do you still keep that photo of your dad in your purse? I also remember that little lizard tattoo on your thigh, the one that went wrong at that place in Blackpool and you said you'd never tell your mum or anyone?"

She nodded as she opened her eyes and held him tight. It was him, he'd been there for her all the time. Maybe he'd even sent Imogen back to give her the confidence to take a trip to Turkey, alone.

"Promise me you'll never leave me?" he asked.

"I promise."

"There's one way we can be together forever." She pulled away from his embrace. "There's a storm coming for us. When it comes, we jump. When we jump, you enter my world and we be as one."

"I'm scared Oscar."

"There's nothing to fear. Look out at the sea. We'll look fear in the face, together."

Gripping his hand, she stared out at the bay. She heard the silence of the sea, followed by the rumble of the wave as the lights went out when the tsunami reached the moon. It was larger than the mountains, larger than anything she'd seen. The wave roared as it neared and crashed.

"Jump now," he shouted as he let go of her hand and she jumped off the building. She made a grab for him but he'd let go. She was falling alone to her end. The wave consumed her, and she closed her eyes.

Silence eventually forced her to open her eyes. There was no water, there was no wave, nothing but the stillness of the night and the goat's bell as it passed by. As she lay in a heap on the ground below she watched as Oscar kneeled beside her. She tried to speak but her breath had gone. She tried to move but none of her limbs responded. She choked as her last few breaths were being spent. She smiled as her and her love would be together forever more. Oscar leaned up and crawled onto her chest, pressing the last few breaths from her body. Just before her vision gave up, she saw his face contort as he let out a painful wailing sound.

"Ludicro has your soul," he said as his face turned from that of Oscar to that of an impish, wart covered being.

*****

The demonic creature forced his hand in her mouth and down her gullet, then he dragged the light from her body before placing it in his satchel. "Anything for love, they do it all," he said as he danced away into the darkness, leaving Lydia's lifeless, broken shell behind. "My power, your weakness."

*****

I am he,
I am she.
I am it,
But never me.
Who you need,
That is me.
Always here,
Near death, you'll see.

The End

The Curse of Cassia
By
Vanessa Morgan

Mandy

She gripped the knife in her hand. She was breathless, but needed to run; she wasn't safe yet. Her head was pounding and brambles reached out for her as she ran, catching her clothes, trying to stop her. The sky was getting dark. She stopped to catch her breath, clutching a tree trunk. No sound, then a rustle in the undergrowth. She turned. There was a slight hesitation and then she felt the knife plunge into soft flesh.

Mandy's eyes flew open. There it was again. That face. But who was he? He was no one she had ever met before, but his face was familiar. And he was there in every dream she had. Or was he? The face sometimes seemed different, and yet the same. Sometimes laughing with her like an old friend, but sometimes chasing her. But was he chasing her, or was it someone else chasing her. The dreams were getting more confusing and more violent. Why?

She turned to look at the clock. Five minutes and the alarm would be going off and then two weeks of bliss. A quick shower and a coffee and she would be off to the airport to catch her flight to Corfu.

Loukas would be meeting her at the airport. Her gorgeous Greek boyfriend who had stolen her heart with his sparkling eyes, dark hair and brilliant white smile and in the short time she'd known him, he'd become a vital part of her life. So when he had invited her to join him at his villa in Corfu she hadn't hesitated. But he was going for a month and she had only two weeks' holiday time left to take, so she had no choice but to travel alone to join him.

The strange thing was that the dreams had only started after she had met him. And even stranger, sometimes, just sometimes, the faces in her dreams looked so much like him. And yet they weren't him. The alarm buzzed and Mandy climbed out of bed.

She left on time and the journey to the airport took the normal twenty minutes. The car park was full and at first she was worried she wouldn't find a place but on her second time of circling she spotted a space she'd missed. A short walk to the bus stop and a short wait with another couple, and then she was in the airport joining the queue for check-in. Jostling with the usual crowds, she was motioned through security with no problem. She'd learnt her lesson before and made sure she wasn't wearing an under-wired bra.

The plane wasn't full but after taking her window seat, another couple sat beside her. She hoped they weren't too chatty, it was an early flight and she just wanted to doze.

The skies below them were clear and after having slept a short time Mandy turned her head towards the window and saw they were flying over the Alps. She looked down on the snow-capped mountains and green valleys and started to feel strange. She felt someone looking at her and there in the aisle she saw her, a woman with long black hair and dark piercing eyes standing staring at her.

The woman smiled at her but Mandy didn't have time to think, to say anything or move, because suddenly she was falling. Was she falling? Or was the plane falling? What was happening? She squeezed her eyes shut and waited for whatever was going to happen. There was panic and screaming all around her and loud noises from the engine, then everything went quiet. She opened her eyes.

She was lying on soft grass, surrounded by mountains. The sun felt warm on her face, and her ears were filled with birdsong. Lifting herself up, she looked around. There was no debris, no bodies, nothing, she was all alone and way up above she could see a plane flying overhead.

Mandy stood. She shivered and willed herself to wake up. This had to be a dream but it felt so real. The sun shone in her eyes but peering against it, she could see the silhouette of a figure. She strained her eyes and made out the form of the woman from the plane. She was standing some distance away, motionless. Then she started walking towards Mandy. Mandy froze. She couldn't move. Her heart, which was already pounding, beat even faster. The woman, who was now very close to Mandy, stopped. She reached out and took Mandy's arm. Her hand was ice cold and Mandy felt the chill run through her entire body.

"You know what to do don't you," the woman said. Her voice was sharp and rasping. "You have to help me."

"Who are?" Mandy stuttered

"Revenge. It's all about revenge."

"Revenge?"

"Yes. Revenge. You have to kill him."

"Kill who?"

The woman grinned. "Loukas, of course."

"What?" Mandy uttered. Her voice almost failing her.

"Loukas must die," the woman said. "Like all the others. And you have to kill him. It's the only way."

"No ... no ... no!" Mandy sobbed at first before her voice broke out into a scream.

"Are you alright?" Mandy opened her eyes. The air stewardess was bending across to her and the couple sitting next to her were looking concerned.

"Can I get you a drink?"

"No, sorry ... sorry I was having a bad dream."

The air stewardess smiled and left. The couple carried on reading their books. Bad dream was an understatement. Kill Loukas? Why on earth dream such a thing? Mandy looked back out of the window and saw the coast of Italy below her. "Please don't let me fall into the sea," she whispered to herself.

The sea stretched below until they reached the heel of Italy which they followed down to the island of Corfu. She felt the plane dropping but this time it was real. They would be landing soon. The sea came closer and closer until they hit the runway on the edge of the coastline. The plane quickly came to a halt on the short runway and taxied towards the small terminal building. She'd arrived, but her arrival brought a very strange feeling of uncertainty. She wondered if she had made a mistake coming here. The woman in her dream and her demand had frightened her. Kill Loukas. Mandy shivered. There was something else about that woman. At first Mandy couldn't think what it was and then she realised. "Apart from the long black hair she looked a lot like me."

Walking into the airport was unreal, so informal. Straight off the plane, across the tarmac and through a door. She flashed her passport at the guard who just seemed to want to get back to whatever he had been doing before the plane landed. She entered a small terminal building and there was Loukas. Arms outstretched she ran to him. She hugged him tighter than ever before which seemed to surprise him.

"Hey you okay?"

Mandy pulled away and looked at him. Yes, his face really did seem the same as the ones in her dreams. Then over his shoulder Mandy saw her. The woman, her long black hair blowing in the breeze which blew in through the doorway. She turned and smiled then disappeared outside.

"You were on time," Loukas said as he took Mandy's arm and led her out of the building. Her eyes darted around the concourse outside. The woman was nowhere to be seen. "I've missed you so much." Loukas was saying. "Hey are you listening to me."

"What. Oh yes sorry. Just a bit tired. Early morning and all that. Had a bit of a sleep on the plane but not long."

"Well come on it's not too far." He stopped and looked at her. "I love you," he said.

Mandy never thought she would ever hear anybody say those words to her with such feeling. He meant it, he really meant it. This really was love. She could see it in his eyes and feel it in his grasp as he took her hand and led her over to his car. It should all have been so romantic but part of her just wanted to pull away and run back to the airport and take the plane home. She had such a bad feeling. Then the warm April sun hit her face, so different from the clouds she had left behind in England, and Mandy tried to forget her fear.

"I did tell you I'm about an hour's drive from here, didn't I?"

"Yes I'm looking forward to seeing the countryside."

"We'll go along the coast road. It's quite spectacular in some places."

And he was right. The road certainly was spectacular in some places. Sharp hairpin bends circled along the mountains which came down to meet the coast. Below she could see small bays with waves lapping on the rocks which sheltered the secluded coves. With the sun shining through the window she started to doze as the car gently hummed along the uneven road. She swayed as Loukas expertly negotiated the bends and bounced as he unavoidably hit a pothole. Suddenly the figure appeared from nowhere, standing in the middle of the road. Mandy screamed as they hit him and she saw his face as he was flung over the bonnet of the car. HIS face. She squeezed her eyes tightly shut, unable to look. "Stop, stop. You've hit him!"

Loukas swerved the car onto the side of the road. "What's wrong?" he cried.

"You hit him."

"Who?" Loukas asked, horrified. Mandy jumped out of the car and ran into the road, narrowly missing being hit by another car, the driver of which was frantically banging on his horn. She looked back down the road. There was nothing there.

Loukas grabbed her and dragged her back to the car before she could be hit by another angry motorist. "What are you doing? What's wrong?"

"But that man … in the road … you hit him."

"Mandy I haven't hit anyone."

"But I saw him, his face …" Mandy turned to Loukas and it was almost as if she was looking into that same face.

"Come on, get back in the car. You were dozing, it must have been a dream. As you said, with the early morning flight you're still tired."

For the rest of the journey Loukas could sense Mandy was disturbed but he left her quietly to her thoughts. He loved her and was so pleased to have her at his home. He had to make a decision while he was on vacation whether he was going to go back to England to stay or return back to the island. That decision would depend on Mandy.

His house was high on a hill overlooking the sea. Other houses were dotted about, both on the roadside and along the hillside. Some, like Loukas', were well-kept smart houses. Others were derelict. It was strange to see these different types so close together.

And so the holiday began. From Loukas' house it was possible to walk down to the small beach but better to drive down there and park on a piece of rough ground. The sea was inviting, calm and warm, and sheltered. The sand was soft and they spent the first couple of days just lying there, swimming, reading, dozing and eating and drinking at the small bar above the beach. The people were friendly and Mandy felt totally relaxed. She hadn't had any dreams during those first two nights. There had been no sign of the woman and the man who had supposedly thrown himself in front of Loukas' car had been forgotten.

They were sitting eating lunch after spending the morning on the beach. "I've got a meeting to go to this afternoon," Loukas told her.

"You never said anything before."

"No, I've been trying to get out of it but can't."

"What is it?"

"Oh a family thing. I would take you but ... well I haven't told the family you're here."

Mandy looked at him. She hadn't given a thought about meeting his family but now he'd mentioned it she thought it seemed the obvious thing to do while she was here. "It's just they're a bit ... well, a bit wary of foreigners. They didn't want me to go to England in the first place. Was worried I'd meet an English woman." Mandy looked at him and frowned. "Yeah and I have ... but they hoped for a nice Greek woman."

"Well everyone I've met here seem so friendly, why aren't your family like that?"

"Oh something happened years ago and it's just made them a bit wary-"

"What was it?"

"Oh nothing you need worry about." He signalled to the waiter to bring the bill. "Anyhow what do you want to do? Stay here or come back to the house."

"I'll go back with you. I can always sit out on the patio," Mandy begrudgingly replied. Loukas left as soon as they arrived back. He said he didn't know how long he was going to be but he'd be back before evening. After sitting in the garden for an hour Mandy started to get bored. Tomorrow she was going to ask Loukas to take her around the island. It would be the fourth day of her holiday and although she'd enjoyed relaxing on the beach she was now starting to feel fidgety. She normally wasn't a beach-holiday type person, she liked to do things. Go for walks, visit places and explore. So with that thought in her mind she decided to go and explore and take a walk around Loukas' neighbourhood.

His house lay back off the main road to Zassiopi. A few yards away was the turning down the hillside to the beach. She'd also noticed another road leading off that, so thought she'd go and take a look around there. Just in case Loukas came back, she left him a note telling him where she was going.

The road led down among the olive groves and was nicely sheltered, making it ideal for walking on a hot summer's day. The flat pathway and glimpses of the sea through the trees suggested that she was walking in a line along the coast rather than heading down to the sea. Somehow it all seemed familiar to her. Perhaps Loukas had described it in such detail, she knew it as if she had been there before. Or had she dreamt it? She passed a few houses, but nobody seemed to be about.

"Mad dogs and Englishmen," she thought and smiled. "So true," she agreed. After a pleasant walk she came to a church. Again it seemed so familiar and she was drawn towards it. It had probably stood there for a hundred years or more. Old buildings fascinated her so she went under the coloured archway to take a look. The church was more colourful than those back home with its brightly painted walls. It was locked so she started ambling around the graveyard.

The tombs were all packed in tightly together. Large monuments crammed with Greek words and photos of the deceased fixed into the stone with little frames and glass. Mandy felt herself being drawn to one side of the cemetery and down one path in particular. At the end a bright white tomb was gleaming in the sun. She looked down at it. It was a young man's grave where a bunch of nearly dead flowers lay, but the face in the photo she knew so well. It was him; the face in her dreams. Horror-struck. Her eyes scanned the words and despite the Greek lettering she could read the name. Demetri Nikitas. Loukas' family name.

She stepped back in shock; at the same time feeling that someone was watching her. She turned to see an old man standing quite close behind her. He held a fresh bunch of flowers but on seeing her, dropped them. He stared as a look of terror gradually covered his face. She stepped forward to speak to him, wondering what was wrong and wondering if he could tell her anything about the young man in the grave. He backed away from her, seemingly muttering something under his breath, almost saying a prayer. Then hobbling away as fast as he could, he left the cemetery.

Elizabeth

Blood was everywhere. She was covered in thick red gore. As she ran to the beach she could hear the lapping of the sea. Her toes soon felt the trickle of gentle waves.

She ran further into the sea, cleansing the blood from her. Waist deep, she stood listening to the waves and looking up at the bright full moon, then she leant back and let the sea take her.

Elizabeth shot up in bed. She could almost feel herself choking. She'd been having the same dream regularly since they had arrived in Corfu. But that was the first time she had felt the drowning sensation. Before, she had always woken, looking up at the full moon. The family had arrived in Corfu a few months earlier after her father had taken up a position working for the British Consulate. His office was in the centre of Corfu Town but the family had chosen to live in a secluded house just outside Kassiopi. It was a beautiful area but at first Elizabeth had thought how bored she was going to be. But then she had met Demetri.

His family owned olive groves which lay on the hillside around Kassiopi and Elizabeth and Demetri spent their time walking these hillsides, or visiting the coves below, and swimming in the clear blue sea. Today they were visiting his grandparents in the almost deserted and derelict town of Old Perithia.

"We keep telling them they should move like everyone else but they've lived here all their lives. It is derelict. But in a charming way, it's peaceful," Demetri told Elizabeth.

"I think it's a strange place. Well why has everyone just left their homes and moved away?"

"They came here first of all to be safe from pirates that looted the coastal towns. Now because of the tourism in the coastal towns everyone wants to move back."

"Yes but to just leave it so derelict."

"Perhaps it's haunted."

Elizabeth shivered. "Is it?"

"Well it is said that a witch lived here many, many years ago."

"A witch?"

"Yes but I'm going back a bit."

"What happened to her?" Elizabeth asked.

"Don't know. I think she just disappeared."

"Well that's what witches can do, can't they. You know just jump on their broomsticks … ?"

Demetri looked at Elizabeth and grinned. "Now don't be silly."

But despite her joke Elizabeth didn't feel she was being silly. She could feel a chill down her back and was sure someone was watching her. There was something lurking in these empty houses; she could feel it.

Demetri's grandparents couldn't speak English so Elizabeth just sat and listened as Demetri chatted with his grandfather, translating bits and pieces so Elizabeth could be included in the conversation. But his grandmother just sat and stared at Elizabeth. She looked so suspiciously at her that Elizabeth began to feel uncomfortable. Suddenly, still staring, she said something, repeating it at least three times. Demetri looked uneasy and said something to his grandmother in harsh tones.

"What did she say?" Elizabeth asked.

"It doesn't matter. She's just a bit superstitious and says you look like someone come back from the dead."

"You're joking. What did you say back to her?"

"I told her to stop it." Demetri stood and motioned Elizabeth to join him. "Come on we'll go now. My grandmother isn't well so gets tired quickly. We'll come back again." He said something to his grandfather who nodded and walked to the door with them. Before they had chance to leave, Demetri's grandmother got up and followed them. Still staring at Elizabeth she spoke the same words again, pointing her finger at Elizabeth. Demetri led Elizabeth through the door.

"Look your grandmother obviously doesn't like me but you're her grandson, you must go back and talk to her. Help your grandfather calm her down. I'll have a walk around. It's not a big place, you'll find me when you've finished. Demetri smiled and kissed her. "Just out of interest, what was your grandmother saying?" Elizabeth asked.

"It's her. That woman."

"Who? What woman?"

"I don't know. Somebody she knew years ago."

"Obviously someone she didn't like very much."

"Well actually it was a woman her brother knew and …" Demetri hesitated.

"Yes?"

"Oh it doesn't matter," he said as he turned to go back into the house.

"Well it does matter. I seem to be only getting half a story and I'd like to know why your grandmother didn't like me, well in fact she seemed frightened of me."

Demetri hesitated. "Her brother was murdered."

"Oh my …"

"Apparently you look like his girlfriend and they think it was she who murdered him. But it'll remain a mystery because they never found her."

"Great. So I'm a reincarnation of some woman from fifty-odd years ago who committed a murder."

Demetri nodded, then smiled. "But I still love you."

"Do you? It's all rather sudden isn't it?"

Demetri placed his hands on Elizabeth's shoulders. "Elizabeth Mitchell I fell in love with you at first sight. What's going to happen when you have to go back to England I don't know? But we'll figure that out when the time comes." He turned and went back into the house. As the door opened Elizabeth could hear his grandmother wailing.

She walked across to a grassy bank and sat down to wait. The sun felt warm but a light breeze kept her cool. Lying back, her eyes began to close. She felt unnerved by Demetri's story. It added to a feeling she'd had for a while that something didn't seem right. The dreams were getting worse. She'd felt a strange feeling of déjà vu since arriving in Corfu. Now, with the show of aggression made by Demetri's grandmother, she wondered how much truth there was in his grandmother's words. Was she reincarnated from some evil murderer? The blood in her dreams. Whose was it? Had she murdered someone?

 Suddenly she was cold. She sat up. A cloud had moved across and blocked the sun. But it wasn't just that. There was an eerie chill about the place. Elizabeth looked around. Everywhere was deserted, then the sun came back out. Just before it blinded her Elizabeth saw something. There was some movement. A shadow by the wall. She shielded her eyes to look. There was a figure. A woman with long black hair. The second Elizabeth spotted her, she turned and walked through a gap between two derelict houses. Elizabeth felt drawn to follow her.

 At the back of the houses was what would have once been a garden. The woman was bending down as if picking something. Then she looked up at Elizabeth, as if she had been waiting for her. Elizabeth thought there was something strange about her. At first she couldn't think what it was, then it came to her – 'apart from the black hair she looks a lot like me,' she thought – and Elizabeth realised she was trembling.

 The woman's mouth was moving but no sound came out. She stood, raised her hand and pointed at Elizabeth. Elizabeth thought she said something. The sound floated in the air and the only words Elizabeth could hear were 'kill' and 'Demetri'. Then the woman turned and walked around the house. Elizabeth was rooted to the spot thinking about what the woman had just said? When she gained her senses Elizabeth ran in the direction where the woman had gone, but she had disappeared.

A shout came from nowhere and Elizabeth jumped with shock. "Elizabeth? Where are you?" Demetri was calling her. As she appeared from between the two derelict houses she thought he looked afraid. "What were you doing?"

"I thought I saw somebody and was taking a look."

"Yes, well it was up there, where people always said the witch lived."

"The witch?"

Elizabeth thought of the woman she'd just followed with her long black hair. "You said she just disappeared," she asked.

"Yes. She was last seen running down to the beach. It's thought she ran into the sea and drowned."

Elizabeth couldn't help thinking it was that witch she had just seen, and she was afraid. "She couldn't still be here could she?"

"No that was years and years ago."

Elizabeth remembered her dream. "You say she ran into the sea?"

Demetri could see the fear in Elizabeth's eyes. "Come on let's go. I think my grandmother has upset you. But don't let her, we all know she's going crazy." He tried to laugh it off but he felt uneasy too. His grandmother's words wouldn't go away. And he remembered the so-called curse which befell the men in his family who met English girls.

The idyllic summer continued and so did the dreams of blood and choking, but now they were different. The woman was there. Standing at the edge of the sea, smiling, her long black hair flapping in the breeze. But one night it was different. One night Elizabeth woke up and there was the woman standing by the bed. She stood in a pool of water as the drips fell from her dress. She had a wound in her side. Wet and sticky as the blood mixed with the water. Perspiration formed on Elizabeth's brow. She wanted to scream but couldn't. Elizabeth stared at the woman, and the woman looked back and smiled.

Then Elizabeth didn't feel afraid anymore. She just felt anger. No words were spoken between the two women but Elizabeth could hear the conversation deep in her head and she knew what she had to do.

She didn't dress she just went downstairs to the kitchen. Opening the drawer, she took out a knife. The woman stood behind her, smiling, then together they walked out of the house.

Elizabeth didn't feel the stones pressing into her feet as she walked along the path. She held the woman's hand as she walked. Occasionally she would look at the woman, but the woman kept looking straight ahead, smiling. She knew that tonight, once more, she would have her revenge. The Nikitas family would once more feel her wrath.

They arrived at Demetri's house. Elizabeth looked at the woman and a wave of anger enveloped her. She knew what she had to do and had no fear.

*****

The stones rattled on Demetri's window. He stirred but in his sleep they didn't register. The second time he woke, wondering what was happening. The third time the chink of the stones did register with him. He got out of bed and went to his window. Drawing his blinds, he was surprised to see Elizabeth standing all alone below his window; barefooted and only wearing a nightdress. Her hands were behind her back, as if she was hiding something. He couldn't understand what was happening. When she saw him she turned her head, almost as if she was looking at someone standing next to her, and smiled.

"Elizabeth?" he whispered, as loud as he could. "What are you doing? What's wrong?" Something must be wrong but she seemed quite calm.

"I need to see you. Please come down."

"But it's the middle of the night?"

"I know but I want to see you," she pleaded.

"Wait a minute, I'll get dressed and come down."

"I'll meet you on the beach," Elizabeth called as he turned from the window.

"No just stay there." Demetri called back. But she had started walking down the track to the beach and he was certain she was talking to someone. He wondered whether to wake his parents. Something was obviously wrong but as they didn't seem to like Elizabeth he thought it was best not to.

Elizabeth felt the sand moving under her toes. It felt soothing. The woman stood a distance away from her. She was always smiling but her eyes showed no emotion at all, until suddenly they seemed to glint and Elizabeth turned to see Demetri walking down the beach.

"Elizabeth, are you alright? What's happened?"

"You don't really love me, do you?" Elizabeth said.

"Yes of course I do. What is wrong?"

"You brought me over here, but you don't really love me."

"Elizabeth I haven't brought you anywhere. What are you talking about?"

"It's the Greek girl you love isn't it."

"What Greek girl? Elizabeth you're frightening me?"

"Just tell me you love me," Elizabeth pleaded.

"Elizabeth I love you. You know I do."

Elizabeth turned and looked at the woman. She spoke. "He's telling lies. He doesn't love you. He loves me."

"How can he love you?"

"Ask him," the woman said.

Elizabeth turned and Demetri was looking puzzled.

"Elizabeth who are you talking to?"

"She says you love her, not me."

"Who does? Who are you talking to?"

He reached out to Elizabeth. He knew he needed to coax her back home. Something was terribly wrong. She needed a doctor. But the pain shot through him like a streak of lightning. He looked down and saw the blood oozing from his body. "Elizabeth. What have you done?" He backed away. He knew he had to get back home. His feet trudged in the sand, he could hardly move and before he reached the trees he fell to his knees. He felt someone standing close by and he looked up and saw there was a woman with long black hair smiling at him. He felt as if he knew her. But where was Elizabeth? "Elizabeth," he called. His strength was beginning to drain and he struggled to turn. He needed to find Elizabeth. Then he saw her. She was walking into the sea. "Elizabeth!" he shouted. He tried to get up but he could feel his life draining from him. He spotted a man, running down the beach. "Help!" he called. The man stopped and looked down at him, then at the women. "You evil witch. How many more? Haven't you got your revenge?"

"I will never have my revenge while there is still a male Nikitas alive."

As Demetris took his last breath he heard the man say - "And what about her."

He was looking at Elizabeth, now waist deep in the sea.

"It's better this way for her. In any case she's English." As she spoke Elizabeth disappeared under the water.

Mandy

Her black hair blowing in the wind, she smiled at Mandy. This time Mandy felt no fear. The woman was her friend. But him? That man she'd seen so many times before, she loathed him. The hatred was so strong, strong enough to kill. But he looked so like Loukas; Loukas the man she loved. But did he love her? He said he did but the woman was telling her otherwise. She was saying he didn't love her. That he never had loved her. That he never would love her.

Mandy's eyes opened. She was shaking. How long had she been asleep? She'd sat in the shade under a tree and must have fallen asleep. That old man, who was he? He'd seemed afraid of her? She stood, knowing she must get to back to Loukas' house. He might be back by now. But before she left she wanted to take another look at the grave. Why? She didn't know. She just needed to.

That face. The face from her dreams stared back at her from his grave. So like Loukas, his eyes seemed to pierce through her.

"What are you doing? I've been looking everywhere for you." Loukas was making his way down the path towards her but Mandy didn't seem to hear him. She just stared down at the grave. "Mandy?" Loukas reached out to her and she jumped back. "Mandy what are you doing here of all places?"

She stared at him. She could hear the woman's voice whispering in her ear, "not yet, not yet."

"Mandy?" Loukas cried.

Mandy turned back to the grave. "He looks so like you."

"Yes he was my grandfather's brother."

"What happened to him? He looks so young."

"It's a long ... he was ... killed."

"Killed? In an accident?"

"No ... well ... actually he was ... murdered."

"What?"

"Oh never mind about it now. It was a long time ago."

"No you're telling me a relation of yours was murdered and you just shrug it to one side."

"Well it's a bit eerie really. It's thought a girl he was friends with killed him. Stabbed him. But then she just disappeared."

"You have to kill him." The woman's voice from her dream came back to her. Mandy stared at Loukas as he continued.

"Look I didn't want to tell you because it's just weird. And the thing is, it's happened before but the first time it was a local girl called Cassia. The family story says she was a witch. A witch can you imagine that? Long black hair wafting in the wind ... Mandy?"

Mandy was trembling. "Long black hair ..." she murmured.

"Well that's what witches look like isn't it?"

"Loukas why were your family worried you'd meet an English girl?"

"Demetri had an-"

"An English girlfriend. Who they thought murdered him," she said knowing perfectly well what his answer was going to be.

"Yes."

"But if that was just a one off ... unless ... as you said it's happened before." Mandy pushed him to one side. "I have to leave Loukas. I have to go home. I can't stay here. It's too dangerous."

"What do you mean too dangerous?"

"It's just a feeling I've got. A dream ... nightmare ... whatever ... I can't stay." Mandy turned to run but stopped. There she was at the gate. Her long black hair wafted in the breeze, and she looked angry.

Cassia

"What do you two think you're doing?"

Paulos and Cassia froze, the olives still in their hands, not knowing whether to drop them and run or stay and face Rouvin's fury.

"Master Paulos I'm surprised at you. You best be going back to the house and keep away from the likes of Cassia Hanas." He looked down at the two children. What would the master think if he knew his eldest son was mixing with the children from the village? And this one of all the girls. Everyone knew her mother was a witch. "Those olives are for the market. Now be off with you," he bellowed.

The two friends disappeared as fast as their legs could carry them. Not stopping until they reached the open track. "That was close," Paulos said as they stopped.

Cassia was indignant. "Why do I always get the blame when we get caught on one of your dare-devil ideas?"

"Because you're a girl," Paulos replied.

But Cassia knew it wasn't that. She was starting to notice a difference between them. The way people looked at her with disinterest, sometimes distaste, but touched their caps to Paulos. She had just seen the look that Rouvin had given her. Almost hatred. But they were still young and still had a few years of childhood left. And if Paulos loved her like he always said he did, they would marry one day, like he always said they would. Then people would have to treat her differently.

One day Paulos wasn't there anymore. She waited for him at their usual spot, but he never came. She went to the big house but it was locked up. She asked where the family had gone but no one would answer her. They just looked down their noses at her and turned away.

Before long she knew that Paulos had left the island. She didn't know where or if he was ever coming back but she still kept going to their spot in the hope that one day he would be there waiting. Sometimes she would sit there all day until evening came and found her crouched on the ground, arms wrapped around herself, quietly sobbing, vowing she would wait for Paulos forever.

The years passed and Cassia still waited for Paulos to come back to the island. Her mother had died and she now lived on her own. No one came near. She was a witch just like her mother they all said. But she had grown into an attractive woman and longed for Paulos to come home and take her in his arms, then one day the whole village was talking. The Nikitas family were returning. But they were bringing a young English woman with them. The woman that Paulos Nikitas had married.

Cassia listened to the gossip. It wasn't true. It couldn't be. Paulos had always said he would marry her. She spent her days outside the Nikitas' house, waiting. When Paulos saw her there he would remember. He would forget the English woman who had bewitched him and run to Cassia's arms. And so she waited until one day the boat arrived bringing the Nikitas family back.

Cassia rushed to the house and was standing on the roadside as their coach came along the road and turned to go through the gate and up their drive. She saw the English woman. She had blonde hair and pretty eyes but a face that looked so like Cassia's own face. She saw Paulos holding her hand and smiling. "Paulos!" Cassia screamed. He turned and looked at her. The same look Rouvin had given all those years ago. Then he looked away as the coach turned into the drive. She went to run after it but the worker who had opened the gate stopped her and pushed her away. Pushed her so hard she fell to the ground.

It wasn't Paulos' fault. Cassia knew that. It was the English woman. She really had bewitched him. They called Cassia's mother a witch, how could they not see it was this English woman who was the witch? She then knew she had to do something to rescue Paulos. There had to be some way. Then she remembered an old book her mother had …

It said the herbs were to be taken from the victim's own garden. She didn't see any problem in getting into the Nikitas' garden. She knew from childhood where some of the gaps in the walls were. And sure enough they hadn't been repaired. Gently, Cassia cut the leaves from the stem. She only needed a few leaves from each plant, the rest could be left to thrive in the summer sun. She heard a rustle from behind her.

"What are you doing?"

She turned to see Paulos and sprang up to run to his arms. At first Paulos didn't recognise her. Then he remembered the girl he had once played with. But he didn't want to remember or to be reminded. He hoped his own children wouldn't be so stupid.

"Oh my darling she has bewitched you. I'm going to free you," Cassia cried out.

"What? Who has?"

"That English woman."

"But she's my wife," Paulos exclaimed.

"You always told me I was going to be your wife."

"Oh come on we were children. We didn't know any better. There's no way we could ever have married." Cassia felt tears stinging her eyes but in her heart she felt anger. She had heard the venom in his voice. She could see it in his eyes. There was no love there anymore. She felt the knife in her hand and lashed out, cutting his arm. "You witch," he shouted. His words pierced her heart like a knife. She raised the knife and lunged at him. She felt the warm liquid ooze onto her hand. Horror struck in his eyes. Horror, shock and fear. He looked at her in disbelief. He slowly fell to his knees. She knelt beside him and cradled his head in her arms. She kissed him and stroked his brow and once again they were children, children playing in the woods. He had fallen over and she was gently soothing him. He looked at her, puzzled. That face? So like the face of his wife.

"Tell me you love me," she said.

"Never" was the last word Paulos ever uttered.

She felt him sigh as the knife plunged into his heart. Suddenly there was a shout and Cassia looked up to see Paulos' father and brother running towards her. She looked at her hands covered in blood and then looked down at Paulos' body. She felt no remorse. All her life she had waited for Paulos, the man she loved, now she only felt anger and hatred. "Your family will never know peace. I will hunt you down wherever you are!" she screamed as she ran through the grounds into the woods. Paulos' brother was close on her heels. She gripped the knife in her hand. She was breathless, but needed to run; she wasn't safe yet. Her head was pounding and brambles reached out for her as she ran, catching her clothes, trying to stop her. The sky was getting dark. She stopped to get her breath, clutching a tree trunk. No sound, then a rustle in the undergrowth. She turned. There was a slight hesitation and then she felt the knife plunge into soft flesh, her soft flesh. Blood ran from the wound in her side but she pushed him away and carried on running. He didn't follow her far. As his knife had wounded her, hers had plunged into him.

Blood was everywhere. She was covered in thick red gore. As she ran to the beach she could hear the lapping of the sea. Her toes soon felt the trickle of gentle waves. She ran further into the sea, cleansing the blood from her. Waist deep, she stood listening to the waves and looking up at the bright full moon, as she leant back and let the sea take her. As she sank in the cool waters her spirit rose. The Nikatas family would never be happy she vowed.

Mandy

"Who are you?"

"My name is Cassia."

"Cassia. The witch."

"I wasn't a witch. They always called my mother a witch. She just knew how to make potions that's all."

"What do you want from me?"

"I've already told you."

"Yes I have to kill Loukas."

"It needs to be done today. Before you go away."

Mandy opened her eyes. She felt different. She felt liberated. But she felt angry. She was angry with Loukas. She should never have come here. What was going to happen was all his own fault. He brought her here. She turned and watched him sleeping. A black curl had fallen across his brow. She flicked it back over his head. "I did love you Loukas. But I have no choice. It's your own fault." She slipped out of bed and crept downstairs. Everywhere was quiet as she made her way into the kitchen. The table was laid for breakfast the next morning. She looked down at the place settings. Which one will I take she thought. Her fingers went down to the two knives placed neatly on the table, she closed her eyes and took one carefully in her hand. Her fingers folded around it.

"Not here," the voice said.

"Where?"

"The beach."

Mandy turned and smiled at Cassia. "I'm sure Paulos loved you."

"Yes he did once. When we were children. Before his family brainwashed him."

"What happened on that night?" Mandy asked.

"I killed him and his brother tried to kill me. But I hid in the sea."

"What about Elizabeth and Demetri?"

"She killed him then joined me in the sea … and the others …"

"And what's going to happen to me … afterwards."

"You have to decide that for yourself. But I think I know what you'll decide." Cassia smiled.

"You think I'll drown myself?"

"Yes."

"But I don't want to. I don't want to die and I certainly don't want to kill Loukas." Mandy felt a surge of strength come between her and Cassia, and put the knife down.

"I won't do what you want me to do. I won't. It ends here," Mandy said, staring into Cassia's face

"Nooooooo!!" Cassia screamed. Her eyes turned black with anger and she flung herself at Mandy who ran out of the kitchen and out of the front door. Cassia ran after her.

Loukas shot up in bed. "Mandy?" She wasn't there. Mandy." No answer. The house was quiet but the dream he'd had, had left him sweaty and shaky. Something was wrong.

He ran downstairs and into the kitchen. The door was open. What had happened to Mandy? He panicked and saw the knives on the table. Picking one up, he ran outside. Cassia stood watching. Smiling.

By now Mandy had reached the beach and threw herself down on the sand. Tears flowed from her eyes. "This isn't happening. This isn't happening," she cried. She could see the sea in the moonlight. She could hear the waves gently lapping on the water's edge, and there he was, standing between her and the sea. Loukas. No it wasn't Loukas. It was Demetris. Or was it?

"Paulos?"

He smiled and started walking towards her. "I tried to warn you," he said. "Please leave now." Then he seemed distracted and his smile disappeared. "This has to stop," he shouted, looking over Mandy's shoulder.

Mandy turned to see Cassia walking down the beach. "No, it will never end," Cassia cried back.

"We were children. We knew it had to end when we grew up."

"But we didn't have to let it end. You could have told your family you didn't want to marry that English girl and that you wanted to marry me."

"No, you and I had gone our separate ways."

"No she'd bewitched you. Hadn't she?"

"No I fell in love with her."

Mandy could see tears in Cassia's eyes. "Cassia," she said. "Let it go. It all happened such a long time ago. Be at peace."

"I can never be at peace," Cassia snarled.

There was a noise further up the beach. "Mandy," a voice shouted. All eyes were on Loukas as he ran towards Mandy.

"Loukas, stay away. Go back to the house." Mandy screamed.

"Mandy what are you doing?" Loukas cried. He ran to her and tried to take hold of her but she backed away.

"I don't know what's happening," he said. "Why you're out here on your own but please come back. I'll take you home tomorrow. Please come back to the house." He reached out to her and Mandy saw the knife in his hand.

"What's that?"

"I didn't know what had happened. Who was out here? I brought it for …" He looked at Mandy as she took the knife from him.

"You shouldn't have brought this Loukas. You really shouldn't have brought this." Mandy reached out to Loukas and kissed him. A long lingering kiss. "I'm sorry," she said.

He smiled. "That's ok. Don't worry. We'll sort this out when we get back to England." A moment later a look of disbelief etched across his face as the pain seared through him.

"I told you, you shouldn't have brought this," she said. Mandy looked down at the blood dripping from the knife as Loukas sank to the ground. Slowly she turned and made her way to the sea.

Cassia

Her long black hair flapped in the wind. Another death. She could smell it. The smell of the tormented spirit reached her nostrils as she breathed it in. It made her feel strong. She smiled. And so her revenge continued. The family could not escape her. Wherever they went she would find them. Soon there would be another. She could feel their presence getting closer. Years were of no consequence to her. They sped by and it was not long before a plane touched down at Corfu airport. Rachel was arriving to work as a travel rep at a resort near Kassiopi. The first person she met was Fabio Nikitas. Her heart fluttered as he smiled at her.

"No …" Fabio thought. "An English girl. No …" He remembered what happened to men in his family who became attracted to English girls. But it was too late. She had already bewitched him …

The End

Agathe
By
Brooke Venables

"Finally, we found it." Ava pushed through the doors of the Skala Museum, feeling the instant relief from the air-con. Wiping her sweaty brow, she turned to her boyfriend, James, in time to catch him rolling his eyes and mouthing a sarcastic 'Whoopee.' Sweat droplets trickled down the flatness of his expression.

"To think we almost gave up looking for a museum, forcing us back into town to relax in a taverna." James curled his lips, mocking Ava as she rolled her eyes at him in return.

"James, I know this isn't your thing but we can't spend all day every day drinking in tavernas. We didn't come all the way to Kefalonia to not see any sights.

C'mon let's get some culture." Ava spied a notice and pointed to it. "That will make you happy, it says free entry." She playfully squeezed her boyfriend's side.

"Greetings, welcome to the Skala Museum, my name is Katerina." Ava turned, startled at the sudden appearance of the 5ft 7 Greek beauty approaching them. Her voluminous black wavy hair tumbled down to her equally voluminous breasts. Her extraordinary large green eyes framed by the longest of lashes.

"Hi... er..hello." James' jaw defied gravity, dropping in obvious appreciation.

"You are very welcome here," Katerina continued, "The museum is small but has a number of interesting artefacts. I will be happy to be your guide. I must see to something first but I will back in a moment to join you."

"That would be great, thank you." Ava smiled.

"Well this museum got much less boring," James whispered to his girlfriend as Katerina disappeared through a door.

"Seriously James," Ava elbowed him in the ribs, "in your bloody dreams. Anyway it's not funny, with everything that happened with Tina back home, your eyes should be firmly on me."

"Always babe." James kissed Ava's forehead.

"Right, let's begin," Katerina burst back through the door, her smile was wide and infectious. "Let me show you first this beautiful statue." She led the couple to a dimly lit, roped off corner. Behind the rope stood an elegant, 5ft marble figure of a robed woman.

"She is beautiful," Ava said, admiring the fine detail in the smooth stone expression.

"This is Agathe." Katerina introduced the statue with the same enthusiasm that she might do with a close friend or loved one, "Legend has it, that around 480 BCE, Agathe lived as a good, gentle and trusting soul. She was wronged by her lover, who one day strangled her, leaving her dead and buried on the hills. The Goddess Aphrodite felt rage against this man for treating a woman he loved in such a way. She took pity on Agathe, raised her up from the earth and cast her in marble, so that all could gaze on her beauty for eternity. But should any man touch the statue, they would become cursed. They would lose their minds - usually ending in suicide to escape the insanity. To this day, men are still too afraid to touch the statue of Agathe."

"I love Greek mythology." Ava stared at Agathe in wonder. "I studied a little of it for my degree to become a teacher. I love telling such stories to my class."

"Are you also a teacher?" Katerina asked James.

"Good God no, all those kids." James laughed.

"He is currently out of work," Ava sighed, instantly regretting mentioning it as James shot her that 'don't go there look.'

"Yes, but not for long," James retorted.

"Come, I have some fine Attica vases to show you." Katerina led the way to the next display.

James took a last look at Agathe, with her slight smile and robes which draped over her pert stone breasts. Smirking to himself he leant over the rope, unable to resist a cheeky grab of the enticing cleavage.

The compact museum didn't take long to look around. After viewing a few more artefacts from the local area and learning about the history of the old Skala fishing village, James had already lost interest. He never did have a great attention span. His thoughts were now entertained with the image of an icy cold pint of beer, with its droplets trickling down the glass.

"It was lovely talking to you today. I hope you come back soon."

The enthusiastic goodbye from Katerina woke James up from his daydream. Well the visit here wasn't all bad, he thought as he shook the Greek beauties hand.

Back outside, James wrapped his arms around Ava's waist. "You know, there was a reason that place was empty of people and was free. It was crap. Can't believe we walked all this way for that."

"James, please don't be negative. I was just finding stuff for us to do. It's not all about drinking and sleeping. We need to do more together."

"Yes but its beer time now right? That's if we can ever find our way back into the town, with all these bloody side streets."

They set off down the hill, trying to retrace their steps. The museum had been difficult to find and not at all signposted. Since their arrival in Kefalonia two days ago, James had been difficult to please. Ava was trying to be patient with him, knowing he disliked foreign travel. He wasn't used to the heat, the food or change in culture. They didn't go away much together but Ava was determined to try and salvage their five-year relationship, even if he had broken her heart. James had said he would do anything to put things right, so had submitted to Ava's plea for a holiday far away from home- and far away from Tina.

"This will do." James didn't wait for a response, taking Ava's hand and pulling her into a lively little bar. A number of customers were sitting outside, laughing and enjoying cocktails. Inside, the latest dance hits filled the light and airy atmosphere. James found a table, whilst Ava got the drinks in. She had also ordered them both sandwiches and bowl of chips.

Ava welcomed the chance to sit down. Her attempts to stay out of the bars for the day had failed but she didn't care, it was late afternoon and right now she was hungry and parched. She savoured a large swig of her cool white wine spritzer. "What's up?" Ava looked at James, puzzled over his disgusted expression.

"Beer tastes like piss," he grunted after forcing the rancid liquid down his throat, "and it smells like someone's died in here."

"I can't smell anything, here pass your beer, let me see." Ava took an apprehensive sip and then a larger gulp. "It's fine, tastes good to me. You're just being a fussy bugger."

The barman brought over the sandwiches and chips. His English wasn't very good but he said sorry as James handed him his beer and explained in a slow-robot-like fashion, that it tasted disgusting.

"That was a bit rude, the beer was fine." Ava couldn't hide her mortified expression.

"Christ, this stench in here is putting me off eating." James held his sandwich to his scrunched up lips. Taking a reluctant bite, he proceeded to gag and spat out the contents. He reeled back as he watched a large slime covered cockroach crawl out from the regurgitated bolus of food.

"What the hell is wrong?" Ava pushed the sandwich around his plate.

"Fucking cockroaches."

"Where?" Ava parted the slices of salami, tomatoes and cheese. "There's nothing there, you are seriously losing it."

James looked again at his plate and saw no cockroach. "But there was a... look I'm not staying here, this place stinks of shit." He pushed his chair away, his aggressive manner attracting stares.

"Fine." Ava gulped down the rest of her wine and hurried behind James, avoiding eye contact with the bemused onlookers.

Struggling to keep up with James' long stride, Ava clung on round his waist. "We are nearly back, let's pick up some beer from the shop and just head back to the apartment for a bit. Maybe cool off in the pool?"

"Yes, sorry babe. I think the heat is getting to me, I'm not used to it." James came to a stop and hugged his girlfriend, planting a kiss on her cheek. They slowed the pace and continued through the pretty town of Skala until they reached the nearest shop to their apartment.

Whilst Ava was looking for snacks to purchase, James went to select the beer. He noticed an elderly lady trying to reach for a jar of pickles from the top shelf of the refrigerator. She was short with a hunched back; wiry white hairs poked through her neat black crochet head scarf. "Allow me." James offered, reaching up for her. Handing the jar to her frail hand, he smiled. Her lips quivered into a smile in return and thanked him. As she spoke, blood trickled out from the corner of her mouth.

"Are you ok?" he rested a reassuring hand on her shoulder.

She tried to talk but more blood seeped from her mouth. She spat a tooth slowly to the floor, then another, and another followed by globs of stringy clots.

"Oh my God, somebody help!" James placed his whole arm around the old lady; her frail frame stumbled, dropping the jar of pickles. The offensive vinegar fumes rose from the carnage of shattered glass, pickles and pooling blood.

Ava heard him shouting, along with two other customers and a shop assistant. They all ran over to find James with his arm around an old lady as she shook and sobbed. "James what's happened." Ava removed James' arm from the lady and placed a comforting hand of her own on her shoulder.

The old lady spoke in Greek and her tone was cross. James looked to the floor and the blood was gone. The blood around the lady's face was gone. Just a smashed jar. "I thought she was hurt," James protested. The shopkeeper began pointing and shouting in Greek. The other customers muttered to each other in German.

"Look it's a misunderstanding, he was ….. must have, oh it's hopeless. James, let's go quickly." Ava pulled James away, holding her hand up apologetically repeating the word sorry to everyone.

"I saw blood. She was hurt. I thought she was..." James clutched his hair as they strode away from the shop.

"James what the hell is going on? This isn't like you."

"I dunno, the heat, the stress, Greek beer? I'm going mad."

"You didn't touch that statue back at the museum did you? She sends men crazy!" Ava playfully punched his arm.

"Shit, I did you know, I grabbed its boobs when you wasn't looking."

Ava couldn't help but giggle. "Daft sod. Look we still have no beer, so let's stay off it. You're not well. We'll cool off in the pool and chill for a bit."

"I love you, you're far too good to me."

"I know." Ava smiled but deep down she really did know. She felt the hurt that he had cheated on her with her best friend, Tina. He said he was drunk, the usual, always blame the beer. He hadn't been himself since he was made redundant. He had become lazy and irritable. He hadn't been very supportive of her getting her new teaching role, a bigger income and new work friends. He was always making digs at her. She had put it down to a pride thing. Desperate to find the man in him she loved again and because he had pleaded for forgiveness, she needed this holiday to find that distant happiness. So far it wasn't working.

*****

After devouring their burgers from the poolside bar and grill, James playfully grabbed Ava around the waist and teasingly nudged her bit by bit towards the pool. The glint in his eye warning Ava of her impending soaking. Squealing, Ava plunged under the water. She resurfaced with a mischievous expression of revenge. James allowed her to pull him in by the leg to join her, laughing as she thrashed him with splashes.

James backed away, accidentally bumping into a petite blonde girl. Ava noticed her large deep blue eyes, which were not too dissimilar to the perfect cloudless sky. James touched the girl's arm apologising, for what Ava felt was, an unnecessarily lengthy amount of time. The girl swam off to join her girlfriends. Ava watched as the girls laughed together. It's no good, Ava realised to herself. James had always been a flirt, but the trust was gone. Jealousy stabbed at her wounded insides and she hated it.

"Where are you going?" James called out as Ava hoisted herself from the pool.

"Back to the apartment, I'm tired." Grabbing her towel from the sun-lounger, she hurried off up the steps to the apartment block.

James soon caught up with her inside. "What did I do?"

"Nothing I guess. Look I'm tired okay. Actually I felt uncomfortable watching you ogling that blonde girl."

"I bloody wasn't."

"James, you were. I can't help it; the trust is gonna take time. You hurt me."

"So you keep bloody reminding me! What more do you want from me?"

"Please, I'm not fighting. Can we just stay in this evening and be on our own?" Ava looked at him pleadingly, hoping for him to just hold her and reassure her that she is all he wants.

"Stay in? Are you bloody joking? That is all we bloody do at home. You're always too tired or busy fucking lesson planning. You think that I've changed, look at your bloody self. All you go on about is teachers and teaching blah fucking blah!" James stormed into the bedroom, slamming the door.

The lump in Ava's throat constricted her breath. Gasping, she curled up on the sofa and wept. She buried her head in her arms, unable to think or comprehend what was going on in his mind. She had no idea he felt so bitter towards her. Moments later James reappeared in chinos and a short sleeved shirt.

"I'm going out, I'm on holiday and I'm going out. You coming?" James' icy stare was enough to cool the room down.

"No, I think a bit of space might be best." Ava's voice was raspy.

"Suit yourself." Without another word James slammed the front door behind him.

*****

Pushing his way through to the bar of Captain Jack's Nightclub, James ordered himself a tequila shot and a pint. The music was loud and the lounge was full. Tapping his feet away to the beat, he downed his tequila. For the first time all day he felt good. Finishing his pint, he made his way over to the men's. On his way out he bumped into the pretty blue eyed blonde from the pool earlier on.

She said hi and asked him if he wanted to join her and her friends for a drink. James ordered a round of tequila shots. "Here you go ladies." James lined the shots up with the salt and wedges of lemon. Already feeling lightheaded, James lifted his tequila shot and tipped it over his wrist instead of the salt shaker. The blonde girl fell into him laughing at his mistake. The whole group found it hilarious and downed their shots. James felt alive, surrounded by these fun, attractive girls.

It was now nearing 2am, and James was being held up in a slow dance with the pretty blonde. They gently swayed together over to the wall. The blonde pressed herself against him, pinning him to the wall. She wrapped her arms around his neck and kissed his cheek, moving to his mouth. James kissed her back hard, his hands wrapped around her lower back. She slid a smooth naked leg slowly up his. He was aware of his arousal and pushed her off him. Taking her hand, he led her out into the sticky night air.

They stumbled, giggling down the steps to the beach. A short walk around the rocks led to a small cove. Hidden from view, James pulled up the blonde's skirt, they fell to the sand, laughing. James allowed the blonde to pull at his zip. She released his semi-erect penis; her feverish hands unable to get the organ to extend to its full potential. An unsuccessful attempt at sex left them both doubled over laughing at the sudden awkwardness of the situation.

Maybe the fresh air had started to sober James up because his thoughts went back to Ava. He didn't care. *Stuck up bitch*, he thought, *serves her right. Always nagging me, belittling me all the time. I'm not good enough now she's a fucking teacher. Even put me down to that hot museum guide this afternoon. Why mention I was out of work? Bitch.*

Sitting upright on the sand, James declared he felt like he was going to vomit. His insides gurgled their last attempts to fight the overwhelming onslaught of alcohol toxins. James and the blonde stood up, brushed away the sand and staggered back to the steps. The blonde spotted her friends across the street. Giggling, she blew James a kiss and ran to join them.

Clutching his chest, James was overcome with an intense burning pain. Acid rose and lingered in his throat. Trying to clear his throat, James started to choke. The acidic mucus had solidified, constricting his airway. James' eyes bulged in a desperate attempt to free the blockage, snot poured from his flared nostrils. With one final push from his expanded diaphragm, the blockage was forced up into his mouth. James' bulging eyes streamed with panic as his mouth filled with sand. Collapsing to his knees, on the steps, James vomited volumes of dry sand.

Frantically spitting away the remaining grains, James shook fiercely, crying out. A passing couple approached him and asked if he was okay.

"Too much to drink?" The man said, looking at the sick pooling at James' knees.

"San, s, s, sand," James wept as his eyes focused on the sick puddle. It was just normal sick.

"Think you need to get off home mate, need help?" The stranger offered an assisting arm.

James pushed it away, fumbled to his feet and staggered away silently weeping.

Back at the apartment, James rushed straight to the fridge and downed a bottle of water, rinsing his mouth as he did so. He splashed his face, trying to awaken his senses. Nothing felt real. He wanted nothing more than to lie next to Ava and feel some reassurance. The bedroom door was shut. James punched the sofa as he collapsed to it, deciding he wasn't ready to face his girlfriend. The realisation of what he had done sliced into his soul. He would tell her how much he loved her later, because it was the truth. He needed to regain some self-control. With final thoughts of Ava, he drifted into a deep sleep.

James had only been asleep a couple of hours and was certainly not ready to wake up yet. His semi alert mind was trying to process the weight he felt on top of him. Something was stroking his body. He felt hands smooth over his chest, moving down to his chinos, up and down his thighs. It was the tugging down of his chinos that finally got him to flicker his eyes open. The morning light streaming in didn't make it easy for him to focus. Rubbing his eyes, he tried to lift his head.

The body straddled over his legs, climbed to sit astride his middle. James lifted a hand to smooth away the girl's blonde hair, and recognised her as the girl he had been with earlier that night.

"You can't be here!" James tried to push her off, his sudden rush of senses filling him with panic.

The blonde was strong and sat firm. Lowering her face to meet his, she flashed a sexy smile and placed a finger to her lips to silence him. She softly kissed his lips, stopping for a moment to look into his face. A black fly crawled out from her nostril and then another.

James tried forcing his head away in disgust, but the blonde firmly gripped his cheeks. His protests were muffled when she slid her tongue into his mouth. It snaked down into his wind pipe. Gagging him.

Retching with terrified gasps for breath, James grabbed the blondes face, but his hand just sank into the slushy skin. James' eyes widened with horror as he stared upon the blonde's face decomposing in front of him. More flies crawled from the exposed skull and clumps of rotting flesh. She withdrew her tongue which was now black and dripping bitter mucus onto his face. She made her way down to James' exposed manhood, leaving a trail of clumps of flesh as she slid down his torso. James' lungs expanded forcing out his screams.

Ava shot from the bedroom to find James semi-naked, thrashing his arms about and sobbing loudly. "James, James, it's okay, James stop..." Ava tried to reach out to him but she risked getting struck from his air punches. Running to the kitchen, she grabbed a glass of water and threw it over him. "James stop, it's me Ava!"

"She's gone, gone, she's..." James curled himself up tightly at the end of the couch, visibly shaking.

"James, were you dreaming?" Ava carefully approached him, kneeling in front of him and taking his hand.

"No, she was attacking me, she was on me, she was...she was... Are you real? Stay back!" James pulled his hand back, shielding his face from his own girlfriend.

"James you're not making any sense. It's me, it's just me, please calm down, you're okay now."

James allowed Ava to get closer to put her arms around him. She held him tightly as he wept uncontrollably on her shoulder.

"James, go and take a shower and I'll fix some breakfast, you will feel better for it." Ava could smell the stale fumes of alcohol on his breath and oozing from the pores in his skin. He agreed and feebly made his way to the bathroom. Putting the kettle on, Ava fought back the tears. This is not how she imagined the holiday would be. She felt foolish at the thought, they could work things out. But this? This is not James at all.

Everything that had happened back home made sense. She had been working hard, she had become more tired and boring. Ava wasn't trying to make excuses for James cheating on her but it made sense, it was an explanation. But this? None of this, here in Greece made any sense at all. He had been so desperate for her forgiveness, yet he was now so bad tempered and behaving so erratically.

James reappeared as Ava served up some fried eggs on toast. Sitting down, James slowly pushed the food round his plate. "I'm sorry Ava. I can't eat this. I'm not myself, I can't explain it but I do think I'm going mad. Everything around me smells like its rotting, and I'm imagining things. I don't feel in control. I need help."

"What kind of help? Maybe you just need to stay off the booze?"

"It's not the fucki... look, I'm scared. I'm really scared. What if that statue did curse me? I'm scared to see a doctor in case I'm locked up." Tears threatened to fill his eyes again. James had never felt so vulnerable. 'Can we go back to the museum and ask that guide if there is a way to lift the curse?'

"Do you know how crazy that sounds?"

"We could just go back to pretend we are interested to hear more about it, because it had been so interesting. Please Ava, I know I sound nuts, and I'm asking a lot. Just look at me."

"Well you must be desperate to want to step foot back inside a museum." Ava's attempt at humour fell flat as she looked into the lost expression of her boyfriend. "Okay okay, I'll get ready." Heading to the bedroom, Ava let out a huge sigh. She had come to the conclusion that she just needed to get through the rest of the week as peacefully as possible. She would do what he asked but when they get back to England, she no longer saw a future for them.

At the bottom of the apartment block steps, James froze. Looking over to the pool, he spotted the blonde girl. "There she is, she's the one who attacked me."

"Who?"

"I don't even know her bloody name. I won't let her get away with it." James strode over to the pool before Ava could protest. Grabbing the startled blonde by the arm, James shook her. "What kind of bloody sick trick was that then this morning? You fucking freak. Do you think you are funny?"

"James let her go." Ava pulled him away.

The confused blonde was now surrounded by her friends. "Attacked you? What the hell?"

"Yes I know it was you, you are a sick joke!"

"I didn't hear you protesting last night on the beach?" The blonde stood her ground, looking to him and then to Ava.

"What about the beach?" Ava asked, dreading the answer.

"Not the beach, you bitch. This morning in my apartment, you crept in dressed up and attacked me!" James lunged at the blonde but was pulled back by his girlfriend and blocked by the blonde's friends.

"You have a serious screw loose," the blonde shot back, "control your god damn boyfriend, I have no idea what the fuck he is on about!"

Trying to stop herself shaking, Ava got between James and the blonde. "I don't know what went on last night with you two but right now, James is not well. We need to just leave this now." Ava pulled James away back to the steps. She could hear the girls giggling amongst themselves as they walked away.

"Have I not been humiliated enough James? What did you do with that girl?"

"I told you I'm not myself, I don't know what I'm doing any more. Please I need help. I don't deserve your trust but please help me." Tears fell down his pitiful face. He looked completely broken.

"This is all so messed up. It's not safe for you to be outside. Go into the apartment and stay there. I'll go to the museum alone. Just stay inside ok. I won't be long." Ava watched him skulk inside. Walking away, she let her own tears fall. She didn't know what she was doing, she felt ridiculous going back to the museum but she needed the walk and she needed the space from James.

The museum was empty again. Ava walked straight over to Agathe. *This is so absurd.* Ava had that feeling of someone walking over her grave, she rubbed her arms to smooth the prickly goose bumps.

"Hello, I am Katerina the museum guide."

Ava turned, startled. "Hello again."

"I remember you, yes. Where is your nice boyfriend today?"

"He is not well today, I thought I would come and check out your collection again for something to do. I am especially interested in Agathe."

"Ah yes, she is a great mysterious wonder." Katerina's large green eyes sparkled even in the dim light. "Did your nice boyfriend touch the statue?"

Ava was taken aback with the question. "Actually he did, and he has been acting...er...a bit odd since." It was hard but Ava tried to make light of the situation and managed a strained chuckle. "He can't be cursed though can he?"

"Does he think he is?"

Oh sod it, I can't feel any more stupid. "Actually he does and wonders if there is a cure?"

"Well he is not the first to say they think they have been cursed. Agathe is like a siren, she has a powerful effect on men. I don't know of a definite cure but some people have said that bathing in cave water purifies their soul. There they can seek forgiveness and be well again. It has been practised since ancient times."

"Maybe we could do that." It was no good, Ava couldn't hold back the tears.

"Why are you crying? Are things very bad for you?" Katerina's grin did not mirror her concerned words.

"It's just James has been acting so strange and doing some awful things. It's getting to me, I'm worried."

"I will help you and your nice boyfriend. There is a small cave at the far south end of Skala beach. I will meet you there by the rocks. I am happy to help. He can bathe in the cave's pool for a short while. He may feel better. He may not. Worth a try?"

"I think I will try anything. It is very kind of you. If you are sure you don't mind?"

"I am very happy to help. Be there at midnight tonight and bring a torch." Ava wondered if Katerina ever stopped grinning.

*****

It was approaching midnight, Ava linked arms with James as they strolled along the soft shale beach. Lights twinkled from the town, just illuminating the shadows of the hills of pines in the distance. It was the most peaceful Ava had felt since arriving in Skala. She occasionally gave a reassuring squeeze to James' arm as they walked in silence. She had found him huddled in the corner of the lounge with his hands over his ears, when she had returned from the museum. Raw scratches were visible up both of his arms, where he had clawed at himself. Seeing him so vulnerable saddened her, despite him cheating on her. It was clear that he was mentally unwell, but James was insistent he needed a cure from the statue. If this didn't work, then Ava was going straight to the doctors for advice.

Katerina was waiting for them by the rocks at the end of the beach, like she had said. It was clear to her from James' body language and expression that he was terrified of something. "Come, let's not waste time. You have a torch James? Good. You will need to follow this rock round through the water. It is not deep. You will come to a small cove. You will see a cave entrance. Go inside and there is a narrow gap, but big enough for you. Squeeze through. It is safe. There is a ledge and a pool of water. Not deep. Lie in it for a short while, pray and think pure thoughts. You must go alone. We will be right here.' Katerina nudged him forwards. 'Go, go on."

Ava felt James trembling. 'I'm not sure about this, I think I should-'

"It's ok Hun, I'm going in. I'll be okay. I need to do this." With that James entered the sea, guiding himself around the rock. Stumbling on the big stones under foot, he steadied himself, focusing on calming his breathing.

Shining his torch, James saw the cave opening. Slowly stepping inside, he approached the gap. It was narrow and gently, he felt his way through, breathing in a little to help. The cave was roomier than he expected. The ledge was wide and the roof high enough for him to stand comfortably. He peered into the dark water which pooled before him. The sounds of drips were a comforting silence breaker.

Remaining clothed, James crouched down, hesitantly dipping one leg into the still pool. "Jeeze, it's cold." Leaving the torch lying on the ledge, lighting up the pool, he plunged his other leg in and stood upright, the depth coming to just short of his waist. Shuddering and bracing himself, he lay back to float. It was difficult to think in the freezing water, he pictured Ava's face and thought of when they first met. Oddly enough she had been drunk and had fell into him at Scarlet's Night Club. Funny now, how she is the one going on at him about drinking too much. Ava had achieved so much over the last five years. She never once gave up on fulfilling her ambitions. James realised what a selfish prick he had been lately. He had let his stupid pride put a wedge between himself and the girl he loved so much. The girl that never gave up on him either.

    Splashing the water over his face and smoothing his hair back, James felt ready to get back to Ava and to get back to making a happy life with her. *If she has any respect left for me, I'm going to devote all my time loving her - if she will let me. I will ask her to marry me.* Standing fully upright, James went to lift himself up onto the ledge, but the thing that had just gripped his ankle, pulling him back under had other ideas.

    The pool wasn't deep but James struggled to find his footing as many hands reached up from underneath him pulling at his clothes, pulling him under, using him as a tug of war. Gasping, muffled cries for help were fruitless. Feeling faint, James felt his body being dragged out of the water. At least six corpse-like figures of rotting flesh towered above him dripping with blood. Hissing amongst them, they continued to tear at his clothes, clawing at his skin with bony sharp fingers.

    Paralysed with fear James couldn't find the strength to scream. He had been imagining so much lately, he didn't know what was real any more. He scrunched his eyes shut, praying for it all to stop. The corpses took hold of his legs and arms, pulling him in different directions with such force, that he felt searing pains from his skin splitting at the joints. James had found his scream.

"Can you here that?" Ava said. "Was that a scream?"

Katerina shrugged her shoulders, continuing to grin, admiring her nails.

"I'm going to get him, somethings not right." Ava felt a grip around her arm as she tried to walk away.

"Don't be foolish," Katerina scolded, she was no longer grinning. "Maybe your nice boyfriend cannot be pure after all."

"What? Let me go!" Ava tried to break Katerina's grip but was pushed to the ground.

"He cannot be saved now; you must leave him to his fate." Katerina was leaning over Ava on the sand.

Ava looked up at Katerina and noticed a pendant dangling from her neck. Grabbing it and pulling it closer, she saw that it was moulded into the image of Agathe. "Are you some sort of sick fanatic? Is this all you're doing? You're responsible aren't you? What have you done to James?"

Katerina was grinning again. "I have done nothing, lovely, sweet Ava. Your boyfriend should not have touched the statue."

"The whole curse thing is bollocks. He is not cursed!" Ava scrambled back to her feet.

"That is right," Katerina's smile broadened even more, "James is not cursed, it is you that is cursed."

"What are you fucking on about?"

"James is suffering because he is your lover. He has wronged you. He will continue to suffer as long as you live. The only way to save him is to end your life and he will be free from your curse. Or he could kill himself? But if you live, you may never take another lover as they will all meet the same fate. It is you who is cursed."

Ava couldn't take in what she was hearing, gripping her scalp she screamed in frustration. "This is insane. You are insane!" Lashing out, she grabbed Katerina with all her strength, throwing her to the ground. Not looking back, she ran into the sea, falling over the stony floor, but not stopping. Entering the cave her stomach knotted and she felt sick. The silence unnerving.

"James?" Ava called out squeezing through the gap. Silence. Ava froze. Before her, she witnessed grotesque figures of bone and hanging flesh. They faced her and hissed before melting into the walls of the cave.

James' naked body was lying at the far end of the ledge. She ran to him falling to her knees. His body was lifeless and blood spilled out from his wrists. In one hand he clutched a sharp, flat piece of flint. "James?" Ava stroked his face and shook his shoulders. "James?" Her tears fell, terror clutched at her throat. James was dead. Looking to the cave walls, Ava let out an anguished scream. It was all true, everything James had seen was true. What Katerina had said was true. She had seen it for herself.

Ava held James' head and cried. "You did not deserve this. Not you, not this. No matter what you have done. I love you so much." Katerina's words span around Ava's head. 'It usually ends in suicide to escape the insanity. You are the one that is cursed. All your lovers will meet the same fate.' A hopeless void surrounded her aching heart. Ava took the flint from James' hand. Slicing the stone into her wrists, she hardly felt the pain. She lay her numb body next to James, draping her bleeding arms over him. She closed her eyes and pictured James smiling as they danced together on their first date. The dancing stopped when her heart had stopped.

*****

"Hello!" Katerina burst through the Skala museum doors grinning as she startled the couple standing in the foyer, "You are very welcome here, Sarah and Rob. Sorry I kept you waiting. I am happy to be your guide. Step this way, first let me show you this beautiful statue, her name is Agathe..."

The End

The Cliff House
By
Mark Wallace

It was a rare evening as I drove along the quiet Greek shoreline road towards the cliff-top house I called home. Rare not because of the clear skies still with enough light to hide the stars, nor because of the relaxed calm of the air that held subtle scents of nearby pines and the tang of the sea. It wasn't because my decades old Mercedes convertible purred contentedly along the stretch of uncharacteristically smooth asphalt, or that I had no financial worries for the foreseeable future.

    It was rare because, for once, I was in a good mood.

    The feeling had crept up on me without being noticed and it was only now I realised it had settled. I even had a small smile on my face. I altered the rear view mirror and took a glance to remind myself of what that really looked like. I tried a grin and against the faint tan of my clean shaven face my teeth seemed to shine in the fading light. I reckoned I could pass for mid-forty which was considerably younger than I actually was. Put that down to the benefits of my lifestyle.

I preferred driving at dusk. My eyesight is good enough that I don't bother with headlights on the smaller roads, resorting to sidelights as a courtesy to other folks who may be around. I knew the roads and there were very few other people in the area.

So seeing a backpack wearing figure walking along the roadside ahead piqued my curiosity. He heard the car, turned and stuck out his thumb in the hopeful manner of hitchhikers the world over, peering intently at the car as I approached.

His lean frame bowed slightly under the weight of his pack. Free from his burden I guessed he'd stand about six feet tall. He was a fit looking guy, if a little thin, and I judged his age to be late twenties.

I had plenty of time to take in his features before deciding what to do. Normally I'd pass by and ignore any gestures that may follow, but right then I had been saddled with the unexpected baggage of my good mood.

Underneath a mop of shaggy hair and dark eyebrows I saw intelligent eyes. He had a strong nose, good cheekbones and a mouth that bore the hint of a smile. He reminded me of a young Mediterranean Sean

Connery. The length of his hair and few days' growth of stubble leant him a handsome roguish air.

He also looked exhausted.

Hitchhiking - and picking up hitchhikers - can be a dangerous business. He might have had accomplices waiting nearby. Tough, desperate men lurking in the tree-line ready to pounce once I had stopped, but from the look of him I thought that was unlikely. If he'd been a fresh faced young girl alone on this road then my alarm bells would have been ringing loudly for sure, however the fact that he looked capable of looking after himself was oddly reassuring.

I pulled up next to him and he looked over the top of the passenger window at me. Those intelligent brown eyes weighed me up as he spoke haltingly in Greek, asking if I was heading towards the nearby Turkish Border. He had an Italian accent that gave his Greek more of a musical lilt.

"I speak Italian if that helps." I told him in Italian.

"Is it so obvious?" He laughed, relief evident now he could use his native language.

"Tuscany?"

"Close." He smiled. "Umbria, but very near to the western border, so I expect I sound a bit Tuscan."

I nodded slowly. It had been many years since I had last travelled so far.

"I'll open the trunk." I told him, switching off the engine. The faint sounds of the evening surrounded us as I met him at the rear of the Mercedes and used my key to open the trunk lid.

"Thank you, I'm really grateful." There was genuine gratitude in his voice. He hauled the pack off his back and placed it in the trunk space. I noted that despite his weariness he took care that none of the buckles caught the car's paintwork. I appreciated his consideration.

He waited for me to close the trunk lid then offered his hand.

"Bernando Idini." He caught himself, smiled and shook his head, "Sorry - just Ben."

I met his eyes. I could tell that although he was thankful he was trying to work out who I was and why I had stopped for him.

Most times I avoid shaking hands if I can, however I made an exception in his case. His grip was firm and his hands were hardened from recent manual work.

"Leo," I said, keeping my voice polite but cool. Ben nodded his thanks and we both got into the car.

"I really do appreciate this," he said as I started the car, "it's good to be getting a bit further down the road whilst giving the legs a rest."

As I drove I glanced at him. Ben made no comment about me driving without headlights on, and as I looked at him again I saw he was more tired than he'd first appeared.

"Not the best road to hitch on." I commented. "Nor the best time of day."

"Yeah," he murmured, "beautiful scenery though. Great beach and the sea just over there..." He tailed off as his eyes wandered over the shoreline.

I let him sit quietly as I drove. A jumble of thoughts and ideas had begun to writhe in my head. I pushed them aside knowing it wouldn't be long before they returned.

"Been travelling long?" I asked. The words seemed to bring him out of his reverie and he looked over at me.

"Hmm? Oh, about five weeks." He yawned, covering his mouth. "Sorry. It's been a busy few days."

"Sounds like there's a story there. Go on." I kept my eyes on the road ahead.

"Yeah. That's true enough." His laugh was short and did not contain much humour. "Short version is that I lost some travelling money, so I've been working whenever I can to build it back up. Most of it has meant some very long days and plenty of backache. But I should have enough to get me through Turkey now."

"So what's the plan? What are you doing?" I asked softly. I was genuinely curious about what this young guy was doing.

"I'm circling the Mediterranean, making notes about the landscape, the architecture and the people - for a book. It's mostly architecture, that's what I studied..." Again he tailed off.

I looked at him and gave a slow approving nod.

"Research the hard way."

"The best way I think. The experience of being there makes it real and I'm hoping that will come across with what I write." He yawned again.

I realised I was becoming one of those hitchhiker interrogators, but wanted to know more for various reasons.

"Have you been able to keep in touch with your folks back home? Let them know you're okay from time to time?"

Ben was silent long enough that I thought he might have fallen asleep. I glanced across at him but he was awake and looking through the windscreen. After another moment he spoke.

"No need." He shook his head. "I've no need to let anyone know." He turned to me, his smile tight and a bit forced. "That's why it's an ideal time for me to do it. No responsibility to anyone except me anymore."

There was another story there as well but one to leave alone for now.

We were approaching a minor road junction but I was reaching a much larger personal turning point. I slowed the Mercedes and paused, looking at Ben.

"If you don't mind me saying I don't think going to the Turkish border tonight is a good idea, neither is camping out in the wild. You look like you need to get some proper rest. Use my guest room for the night and I'll drop you off tomorrow. Sound okay?"

Ben was quiet for a couple of seconds and I thought he might turn down my offer, which would have been unwise.

"Thank you. That's really good of you - you'll have to let me pay my way."

"Don't worry. I'm just happy to help out," I lied.

I turned the car along the road towards my house and we drove on in silence.

My good mood had finally dissipated, but that didn't matter. I was back to normal and was interested in finding out more about Bernando Idini.

He intrigued me, which probably wasn't a good thing.

*****

My current home was built nearly five hundred years ago with stone quarried from around the region. It is a square and sturdy design that is set on, and in, a section of rocky cliff that rises some twenty metres from the waters below. From the sea it has the look of a squat castle thanks to its blocky appearance but inside I have made it a far more comfortable home than its appearance implies.

It is known simply as The Cliff House.

I liked that it does not appear ostentatious or grandiose, though there are more rooms inside than one would expect. It is a design that incorporates spaces carved from the rocky cliff beneath it, and there is even a small sea cave I use as a boathouse complete with space for a modest launch.

However, the view greeting Ben as we drove up the slight incline towards the gate was that of the upper floor of the house rising above the olive and lemon trees in the surrounding grounds. I touched the remote as we approached and the iron gate slid smoothly aside. Ben looked around taking in what he could of the place as I parked the Mercedes under a stone shelter separate from the main block of the house and switched off the engine.

"Welcome to my home."

Ben turned to look at me.

"Nice place," he said, plainly impressed. I was vaguely annoyed because I had no desire to impress him, then I remembered he was a student of architecture so he was probably appreciating the simplicity of the building and its surroundings.

I thanked him modestly, got out of the car and opened the trunk. I lifted out his backpack without thinking and handed it to him. As he took the weight I caught his odd look.

I'd handed it to him with one hand and I could tell he was wondering how I'd managed to do that so easily. I let it pass and smiled reassuringly.

"Come on," I said. "Let's get you settled in."

We walked over to the main door. Ben remained quiet as he followed me. I opened the door and gestured for him to enter. He gave me a brief smile of thanks and went inside.

We were met by a man striding across the cool marble hallway towards us. He had an air of athletic vigour and tight muscle and that was at odds with his cropped grey hair and deeply lined face.

"Vitaly, we have a guest." I greeted him in our native Russian.

Vitaly nodded, his face showing no emotion as he reached for the backpack Ben carried.

"I will take it," rumbled Vitaly. His Greek was close to fluent yet retained the harder edge of his Russian accent, but he spoke clearly enough for Ben to understand.

"Thank you, it is okay. I will carry," replied Ben. Vitaly shrugged and looked at me.

In Russian I quickly explained to Vitaly about Ben.

Vitaly Pogodyan was dependable and trustworthy. I paid him far more than he needed, considering his tastes were simple. The only other member of my household was Fyodor, another fellow Russian and a broad slab of a man who filled the role of cook, amongst other duties. However, it was Vitaly I trusted the most, and we had developed a mutual bond that was the nearest thing to friendship I'd had in many years.

I turned to Ben and told him that Vitaly was my assistant and the equivalent of a modern butler. It wasn't too far from the truth, if it meant the butler could also easily kill you with his bare hands. Vitaly had served in the Russian Special Forces, the Spetznaz, before I'd recruited him.

Vitaly beckoned to Ben.

"You come with me." He said using slow and deliberate Greek as their common language.

Ben smiled again and nodded his thanks at me. I returned the smile and nod, telling him I'd see him the following morning after breakfast.

I watched them both leave. My smile faded and I went out onto the cliff-top patio where I watched the sea grow restless underneath the light of distant raging stars.

*****

The following morning had the usual bright clarity for which Greece is renowned. The sea had calmed and it promised to be the sort of day that made fat tourists sigh with wonder and sweat before turning red under the heat of the sun.

I sat in the shade reading a popular thriller novel and simply enjoying the warmth. Vitaly sat on the stone wall of the patio nearby, clad in a loose cotton shirt and pale chinos, smoking his fourth cigarette of the day and looking out over the Mediterranean.

Ben turned up on the veranda in the middle of the morning wearing some shorts and a long blue cotton shirt. He'd used an elastic band to pull his damp hair back and I noticed he had taken time to shave.

I smiled, genuinely pleased to see him and the feeling genuinely surprised me.

"Sleep well?" I asked.

"Oh yes!" He nodded. "I really needed that. Thank you Leo."

I thought for a moment he was going to shake my hand or clasp my shoulder but thankfully he didn't.

"Breakfast?" I asked. "Cooked, continental? What takes your fancy?"

Ben appeared unsure of what he wanted faced with so many potential options, then quickly came to a decision.

"Something simple. Yogurt, fruit. Maybe a bit of honey? That would be great - thank you."

I nodded at Vitaly and he disappeared inside.

Ben sat in the chair adjacent to me. He sighed. It was a contented relaxed sound.

"Again, I really do appreciate this. If there is anything-"

I cut him off. "Actually yes there is."

He looked enquiringly at me as I laid the book on the table and lowered my tinted glasses.

"I have a suggestion and a request: Stay for a few days whilst you begin writing." Ben cocked his head, momentarily puzzled. I went on, "You could do with the break and the stability of somewhere to use as a base. Turkey is close by so you can spend some time there easily enough. And when you are ready to continue your journey further you'll feel better able to face it and move on."

Ben looked away, studying his hands and rubbing absently at the callouses. He was silent for a long moment before looking back up at me.

"Why would you do this?"

"I was young once. Had dreams but no backing. Had to do everything myself. I see a similar situation with you so I'd like to help in some small way." I lowered my glasses and stared at him. "But in return I do expect good conversation of an evening as payment."

"Of course, I'll do my best." Ben tried to suppress his smile and failed. Then an unexpected shadow of concern crossed his face. I read all I needed in that subtle, unsure, look and shook my head.

"Such an issue of modern times." I sighed. "Rest easy Ben. I'm not that way inclined. Intelligent company is enough."

There was an uneasy quiet between us that I had to break.

"Unless you have fishnet stockings in your backpack and fancy shaving your legs, in which case..." I waggled my hand showing that I might be tempted. Ben laughed. I grinned at him. It was false but looked real enough.

"Sorry, no stockings, but getting some clothes washed would be good," said Ben.

I told him that wasn't a problem, which coincided with Vitaly returning with Ben's breakfast.

We spent the rest of the morning discussing Mediterranean architecture and by early afternoon I'd persuaded Ben to use the guest computer in the small library to get some of his trip notes written and stored online.

I gave him a brief tour of The Cliff House and he was fascinated by the number of rooms that had been carved out of the rock underneath the house. I didn't show him everything as we went down through the three sub levels. It was my house and therefore my prerogative as to what he had access to and Ben was polite enough not to enquire what lay beyond locked doors. Anyway I could tell that the highlights of the place for him were the library and the sea cave where the launch was moored.

Whilst doing this I had Vitaly search through Ben's belongings. Not that I am paranoid, just cautious and do not take to trusting others easily. I wanted to make sure he was who he said he was.

Tour over, I left him in the library at the computer, arranging to meet on the patio for supper later.

Part of me wanted to do exactly what I'd told Ben, to help him with his project and to allow him to begin preparation for the next leg of his journey. In reality I knew it probably wouldn't end like that.

It never had before.

*****

Over the next few days we began to establish a comfortable routine.

Ben spent a diligent amount of time writing up his notes and storing them in an online area where he would be able to access from anywhere in the world. I may be old but it is something I understood and could relate to. It was a good idea.

We dined together of an evening. His conversation was erudite and engaging. I ate little, as is my way, but I enjoyed having him around. He was very likeable and having him around brought a welcome lightness to my day.

On the fourth day I lent Ben the keys to an old Japanese 4x4 I had tucked away in the garage. It worked well enough and gave him the illusion of independence. It was another generous gesture which he appreciated.

He drove along the Greek coast taking his digital camera and notebook, seeking architectural places of interest related to his work. I enjoyed hearing about what he had discovered but we also discussed politics, religion, the world and the universe in general, the conversation finding its own pathway as the topic shifted from one subject to another. Laughter was frequent and even my own was often genuine.

We played cards and I taught Ben how to play Canasta. Occasionally Vitaly would join us, amazing Ben by how much vodka he could drink without any apparent ill effect. Vitaly passed this off as a natural ability of any true Russian.

One evening Ben asked if it would be okay to cross over the border and begin exploring parts of Turkey. The fact he had asked permission pleased me and I readily agreed. I trusted him. I had no reason not to.

*****

Close to the end of the second week I took Ben out on a trip in the Mercedes. It was an evening shopping trip to one of the more upmarket towns along the coast, a place where luxury yachts outnumbered local vessels by a factor of three to one.

I treated Ben to a selection of new clothes. At first the old apprehensions about my motives resurfaced. I picked up on this and we had a friendly but frank conversation in a coffee shop which seemed to reassure him. I was not an older Lothario grooming a potential lover. He needed new clothes, I had the money and considered him to be a friend. It was as simple as that. If he wanted to, he could pay me back when his book was successful. He found it hard to understand my generosity but was grateful nonetheless.

The fact that the smartly casual look suited him so well helped convince him. He also had his hair cut and styled saying he felt the longer, shaggy look no longer matched his new image. I approved. He looked good. Maybe even a little like me.

We indulged in banter together as we caught the eye of many passing ladies, Ben claiming the lion's share of the looks, and the bonds of friendship grew.

I tried to ignore the incessant gnawing of dark thoughts at the edge of my mind. They would get their time in due course but right then I wanted to feel like a normal man.

I noticed Ben's gaze drawn to a jeweller's window and the display of watches arrayed there. Some were bulky and overly masculine to the point of vulgarity, others had a simple elegance that spoke of quality and restraint. All were lavishly expensive and bore well-known names. We discussed the merits of their varied styles and I was pleased to discover that his tastes mirrored my own.

Upon our return to The Cliff House late that evening I presented him with a box containing the Patek Phillipe watch I knew had been his favourite.

He was stunned to silence at first, but when he found his voice he began to protest vigorously. He could not possibly accept such a lavish gift. It was too much. The clothes were one thing, but a watch that must have cost the same as a small car made him feel uncomfortable.

For me the cost was immaterial. I knew it would make it much harder for him to leave. Looking back, I realise that the cold merciless fragments of my damned soul had no intention of ever letting him go.

Eventually he capitulated and accepted the watch. There was a point when I thought he was going to cry. I suppressed a shudder of disgust and the moment passed by.

*****

The evenings passed too quickly. The weeks became a month.

Bernando Idini had become the centre of my isolated world and, though he didn't know it yet, he was mine.

There was no desire to connect physically with him, not in any sexual way you may imagine. I enjoy a uniquely celibate existence and my pleasures lie along different paths.

I remained playing the role of older friend, elder brother or avuncular mentor, as suited the situation. But as our second month drew to a close I knew that this could not continue for much longer.

The hard looks I had from Vitaly also betrayed an underlying concern.

"Sir, you need a distraction." He said, placing a cutting from a local newspaper before me. Ben had left for the day and Vitaly and I were alone in the study.

The article was about drug smugglers migrating to the easy money of people trafficking. The lack of police resources available meant the problem was growing. I bet the authorities had loved the article.

"You know I can find the people doing this," he said meaningfully and I didn't doubt him. I knew he kept well informed about what was going on in the area, in fact he considered it part of his job. I made sure he had access to enough funds to finance any information gathering he deemed necessary, and because he wasn't bound by the same constraints the police were his methods could be very direct.

"Do it," I told him, my voice a harsh rasp.

"Take an evening on the boat," he advised. "You need a break. Alone."

I nodded.

That night I took the steps down to the sea cave and piloted the launch out of the dock and into the smooth swell of the sea. I navigated by starlight, caught fish and let them all go again. If only life could be so simple.

I returned before dawn, docked and slept fitfully on the boat until mid-afternoon.

*****

Ben came back late that evening. He was not drunk but I could smell the scent of ouzo on him. I could also detect that he had been enjoying intimate female company, not only from the faint aroma she had left on him but from his general demeanour.

I let it pass. He was a young man. Even I had been young once and had enjoyed the sensual pleasures that a woman can offer, though I found it difficult to remember now. However, deep down, I felt an angry ember of unreasonable jealousy ignite.

He did not make any mention of her and I did not raise the subject.

The following night was a repeat performance. Less ouzo, more of her. To my senses he reeked of the woman. I found it hard to hide my rage and suppress the violent urgings of those insistent voices inside me. I passed my mood off as nothing more than indigestion brought on by unwelcome news and nothing to be concerned about.

When we sat on the patio together, me nursing a warm glass of red and Ben with a cold beer, the conversation felt forced. There was little he could tell me of his day and his mind appeared to be elsewhere. I could tell he was getting bored with the area and probably my company even though he was still grateful of my ongoing hospitality.

I excused myself earlier than normal and found Vitaly in the kitchen carving chunks of lamb onto a plate. Fyodor, the cook, had left for the night.

"Those men you mentioned?" I asked, looking meaningfully at him.

Vitaly's face remained impassive. He spoke as he carried on cutting the meat.

"Three identified for definite already. More tomorrow if all goes well."

"I want them all," I told him.

He nodded. "Two more days. I will have all you need."

I left him to his meal and took the stone steps down to my room where I lay awake counting the hours, seconds and minutes as my wretched life slowly passed, suppressing the need to scream my frustration into the darkness.

*****

Ben had gone by the time I emerged the following morning and Vitaly was nowhere to be found. I checked the garage. Only the Mercedes was left which meant that Vitaly had taken the spare vehicle. I growled without knowing why and returned inside.

I felt weaker than I should have, which added to the hollow, directionless mood that draped around me like an unwelcome shawl.

The sun was strong today and I decided to avoid it entirely by spending the day in my small home cinema tucked away in one of the subterranean rooms. I locked the door, watched home movies and emptied the fridge of snacks.

By the time Vitaly returned the sun was bleeding its last into the sea and I felt more like my old self. I had a renewed sense of purpose and the path ahead was clear.

Fyodor the cook was in the kitchen preparing some pasta dish. Vitaly sat at the rustic wooden table sipping a cold Mythos beer and chatting with him. When I entered the conversation stopped. Fyodor nodded a greeting before turning back to his work. He was one of Vitaly's men who had been with us for the last five years. He was very good with a knife, and not just in the kitchen.

"Sir," said Vitaly. There was glint in his eyes. Evidently he had been enjoying his work today.

"Busy day?" I asked.

He rose to his feet. "Yes. May I show you in the study?"

I let him lead as we made our way into the small room that was used as much by Vitaly as it was me. I shut the door behind us.

Vitaly went over to a laptop computer sitting on the desk and opened it up. He keyed in his password and selected a folder from the screen displaying the multiple contents.

"Six men," he said. "All within thirty kilometres. All involved. All guilty."

"Just six?" I queried.

He shrugged. "There were seven, but information had to be obtained somehow."

"But it goes higher." I clarified. "They work for someone. The chain goes up."

Vitaly shrugged again. "Of course. But how high do you want to go? You are not Batman."

I smiled. It was an old joke between us.

Anyway, I was really only interested in the vermin on the lower levels. They wouldn't really be missed because they weren't that important.

"I also had a man checking our guest."

My look of interest prompted Vitaly to continue.

"He has taken a liking to a woman in a small town just over the Turkish border."

Vitaly opened another folder and brought up a picture on the screen. It had been taken from some distance but was clear enough to see that it was Ben with his arm around a similarly aged girl. She was dark haired, petite and had a captivating smile. In fact, she looked lovely and I could see why Ben found her so attractive. I wanted her dead. Possibly tortured first, but dead regardless.

Vitaly caught my look and frowned. "The men, Sir." he said as he clicked the mouse pointer, closing the photo of the girl and opening one of a swarthy youth. "When were you thinking?"

There was a moment of silence between us. I guessed Vitaly now regretted showing me the photo of Ben with the girl. When he next spoke it was not as an employee but a concerned friend.

"How long has it been Sir? Maybe these men are exactly what you need right now." He licked his lips and tried to meet my stare. "And maybe it's time for Mr. Idini to move on?"

My eyes narrowed and Vitaly looked away.

"Bernando Idini will be staying a while longer. First, get me two of those men for tomorrow."

I went on to explain the details of what else I wanted.

I heard Vitaly's quiet sigh but he knew better than to question my decision. It was time for him and Fyodor to really earn their money. I turned and walked out of the room. I knew now that the last weeks had been leading inevitably towards the next couple of nights.

The anticipation excited me.

*****

Ben did not return at all that night.

Or the following night.

I was angry but thanks to Vitaly there were other ways to vent my frustration and other tasks to concentrate upon. It was enough to tire me to the point that I slept well.

*****

Ben appeared late the morning after, the old 4x4 rumbling up the driveway like an apologetic dog slinking back to its master.

I was furious but concealed it beneath a mask of concern, enquiring if Ben was alright or if there had been any trouble at the border.

In credit to him, Ben now told me all about the girl he'd met. Her name was Denia, and he had met her whilst she was helping out at her cousin's bar where he had stopped for a coffee. She was an art student, her speciality being the Italian renaissance. She spoke Italian reasonably well, had a wonderful smile and was genuinely interested in what he was doing. He did not need to explain how captivated by her he was.

I sat and smiled and raged inside.

He told me that he couldn't impose on my hospitality any further and went on, thanking me for all I had done for him, but he could not think of anything fitting other than to dedicate his book to me, promising to return once his journey and the book was complete.

I told him to think nothing of it, but if it was to be his last night we would celebrate with a special goodbye meal. Vitaly and the cook had something special lined up for us later. However, until then we'd take a trip along the coast in the launch.

Ben was hesitant but agreed, probably out of politeness and deference to what I wanted to do. He said he needed half an hour to get ready and would meet me down in the cave by the launch.

It was closer to forty minutes later before he finally stepped onto the boat. He seemed troubled and quiet. I smiled at him and piloted the launch out into the calm swell without talking.

The temperature had dropped and the day had become cloudy and overcast. Although I missed the warmth, the lack of direct sun was welcome, even in the shady cabin. Ben sat out in the uncovered rear of the boat. I couldn't tell whether he was enjoying the trip or not and I didn't really care.

Half an hour later I reached the area I wanted and dropped the sea anchor. We would still drift but it would help with stability.

I went and sat opposite Ben, looking at him. He looked up, briefly met my gaze, then looked away.

"Problem?" I asked.

"I'm sure it's nothing." His smile seemed forced.

"Go on."

"I've tried calling Denia but it's gone onto an answering service."

"From what you've told me I expect she's busy at her cousin's bar."

He shook his head. "No, she was off today. I had intended to go back and see her again tonight, but would call if there was a problem and I couldn't make it."

"She's probably in a bad reception area or a cell tower has failed. It happens a lot around here. Give her another try once we're back ashore." I reassured him.

He nodded but took out his phone and checked it again. There would be no signal out here but he did it anyway.

"Now look at that..." I said, pointing out a half crumbled ancient lookout post on the nearby cliff edge to him. I should have done this for him a couple of weeks ago but it simply had not occurred to me until the other night.

For the next couple of hours, I meandered us along the coast, pointing out all the shoreline structures and landscape features I thought would appeal to his architectural nature. He noted them, commented briefly but remained detached.

The distraction caused by this girl, this Denia, infuriated me yet I managed to keep my anger buried deep. The afternoon passed and the light faded as evening approached.

Eventually I steered the launch in towards the house as the sun was setting. The lights in the docking area illuminated the cave making it easy to find from the water. I also saw the flicker of flame from the patio torches high up on the cliff edge that signified Vitaly and Fyodor had returned and their day had been a success. My smile was genuine this time.

I cut the throttle as the boat slid into the cave. Vitaly was waiting for us on the dockside and took the rope that Ben threw to him. Within moments the boat was moored and Ben stepped onto the stone jetty. I shut off the engines leaving only the sound of the water slapping gently at the launch, made hollow by the echo in the cave. Ben was quiet. Whether it was from my own anticipation or not I felt an unspoken tension in the air. Ben pulled out his phone and shook his head with frustration.

"No signal down here," said Vitaly, stating the obvious.

Ben looked at me. "I'll head to the patio, see you there?"

I stepped onto the jetty and told him to carry on. I'd be up in a minute. He needed no encouragement and jogged away striding up the stone steps into the house two at a time.

Vitaly gave me a look that asked if I was still sure about what we were doing. There was no need to speak. We'd been through this before. He had no moral qualms about what I'd had him do - or what was to come. He was simply checking that I wanted to continue.

A slight nod was all it took. Vitaly relaxed.

It would have been trickier, and a little wasteful, to stop now and I knew he would prefer to see my plan though to its natural conclusion.

We followed Ben up to the cliff-top patio. I could see he was checking his phone for a signal. He smiled and pressed a button. Evidently Denia was on speed dial. He held the phone to his ear and waited as the call went through.

A mobile phone began to ring nearby. A bright snippet of some pop track, slightly muffled. The sound came from the kitchen, just off from the patio area. Ben looked at me, a puzzled half smile on his face.

I smiled back at him.

"Is she... I mean Denia - she's here?" He asked, an element of confusion dampening his happiness.

"Vitaly picked her up earlier." I told him, still smiling. "I liked the idea of her being here for your goodbye meal. Thought it might be a surprise."

Ben started hurrying towards the kitchen door but Vitaly stepped in the way, holding out a hand to stop him.

"She's downstairs." I said. "Let me take you to her. She's been waiting."

Ben shot Vitaly an uneasy look but turned and followed me back down the stone steps into the carved stone bowels of the house. Vitaly trailed a few steps behind. We descended past the first level, the library and wine cellar, and reached a sub landing with a single nondescript but sturdy wooden door. It was a door I normally kept locked, but not tonight. I opened it and led Ben along the short dimly lit passageway to another door.

"Where is this?" Ben sounded nervous. The trust we had built up over the past weeks only went so far.

"Dining room," I explained. I opened the door and stepped into the darkness beyond. "Come on in."

Ben hesitated, unable to see into the gloom.

Vitaly shoved a Taser into his left kidney and pulled the trigger. The crackle of the electrical discharge was drowned out by Ben's yelp and he dropped to the floor, twitching. I knelt down and injected him with a little Ketamine based concoction of mine and after a few seconds he lay still.

I switched on the lights and smiled at Vitaly. A satisfied smirk crossed his face.

Together we got to work.

*****

It took around four minutes for Ben to fully regain consciousness and by that time we had him stripped and secured to the centre of three surgical tables in the room. He wasn't going anywhere.

"What's going on?" he croaked, his voice almost a sob. "Where's Denia?"

I finished connecting the heart monitoring electrodes and laid a friendly hand on his shoulder. I could see the growing terror on his face and smiled.

"She's here."

His gaze darted around trying to see the room but his head was locked in place so there was little he could make out. There wasn't much to see in any case. Rocky walls and ceiling painted white, the three surgical tables - all occupied, medical equipment - some quite specialised, and a series of sluice drains set into the tiled floor for when things got messy.

"Denia!" he shouted, repeating her name again and again, howling it out with such anguish. He heard her muffled whimper from a nearby table and stopped, looking at me, his eyes a mix of hatred and fear. The heart monitor was set to be silent but the screen trace revealed how panicked he was.

"What have you done to her?" There was such terror in his words. I think he cared for her even more than I had guessed. I let him wonder for a deliberate moment before finally speaking.

"Nothing other than restrain her. She's unharmed."

Vitaly and Fyodor had strapped her to one of the other surgical tables before Ben and I had returned on the boat. She was gagged and blindfolded, but other than that, and a mild concussion, she had not been damaged.

It took him a moment to understand what I'd said. Confusion clouded his face, and then a fierce anger took hold.

"What do you want? What are you doing?" Ben's growing rage started to take the edge off his fear. I didn't mind. Fear or anger was fine with me. Anything that kept the heart rate up and blood pressure high.

I patted his exposed arm. "I like you Ben. I really do. And that's the problem. I want you to stay a while longer."

Ben winced, sucking in a breath, as Vitaly inserted the first of the needles into a vein on the inside of his thigh. He really had no idea what was happening to him and I don't think he knew which questions to ask, and even if my replies were truthful I doubt the answers would have comforted him regardless.

Vitaly inserted another needle and Ben gasped again. Vitaly was no nurse but knew what he was doing despite his rougher bedside manner. However, for me, this was an art form.

I picked up the next needle and felt for Ben's jugular vein. He closed his eyes as the tip slid through his flesh.

It took another two minutes before all the needles were in place and tubes from the relevant machines connected. Ben kept his teeth clenched and managed to bite back his moans of pain during this first part of the procedure. He had done well.

Unfortunately, the experience was about to become far more painful.

I prised open Ben's mouth and Vitaly slipped in a mouth guard. I had learned from experience that the agony usually resulted in the subjects biting clean through their tongue and choking on their own blood and flesh if we weren't careful. Now we came to the part I enjoyed the most. I turned the machines on.

His blood was drawn slowly up the tubes into both devices, expelling any air from the system. The last thing I wanted was for Ben to have an embolism after all the trouble Vitaly and I had gone to. The extraction machine continued to pull his blood, storing it in a series of plastic medical bags. I looked on hungrily as the first bag filled and was sealed.

Ben's eyes fluttered under closed lids and he began to grow pale as his body emptied. The second machine reversed flow, forcing what looked like a darker blood back through his veins. It was a concoction based on my own tainted blood that would end Bernando Idini's current life and begin something new.

As the special blood mix pumped back through his body the heart monitor began to draw frenzied spikes across the screen and his screaming started. Within moments his bladder emptied and he defecated. It was a good sign. It was working. I was pleased.

The whole process would take a while longer so I excused Vitaly. Prolonged screams annoyed him and I could handle things for now. I think he went and had a beer in the kitchen with Fyodor.

I cleaned Ben up and wiped down the steel table. To some it may have been an unpleasant job but I didn't mind, besides it would not have been fair to have Vitaly do it.

The screams had given me a bit of a thirst so I sampled some of Ben's blood from the first bag, pouring a measure into a ceramic cup. It tasted so good, that sweet tint of adrenaline and fear, that I ended up finishing an entire half litre and feeling a little bloated.

Ben screamed himself hoarse after fifteen minutes, his voice reduced to a breathy rasp as the pain of what was pumping through his body continued. His eyes were now wide open and staring unblinking at the ceiling as his body trembled and straining muscles twitched.

The Extraction machine stopped, the cycle complete, and I decided to shut off the one supplying the new blood a little early. I didn't want Ben to be too full to begin with. I wanted him to be hungry.

I removed each of the needles in turn and dressed the puncture wounds to avoid any unnecessary leakage. Ben's tremors made it difficult but not impossible. My combined strength and dexterity is such that I was able to hold each area still while carrying out the task.

When I had finished I stroked his arm.

"Soon my friend. Very soon." I reassured him. "Not much longer now."

Ben's eyes swivelled to lock onto mine. Blood vessels had ruptured turning his sclera a shattered red. There was less fear there now. A bit less Bernando Idini. A bit more me. I smiled, satisfied. I was looking forward to the next part although I did feel some slight trepidation as well. I checked the clock on the wall. I calculated that Ben would need another half hour. The change was not a quick one.

I sat and watched and waited while muscle deep shudders ran through the man that had been Bernando Idini.

Gradually, over the next ten minutes the tremors subsided and he lay still.

I heard Vitaly's footsteps along the corridor before he came back into the room, closed the heavy door and stood next to me.

"Is he ready?" he asked.

"Nearly."

I got up and went over to one of the wall cabinets, taking out another gold plated cup and a plastic half litre bag of blood. This was neither Ben's nor my blood, nor was it donated from Vitaly or Fyodor. It came from the still figure that lay under a plastic sheet on the third table. One of the criminals whose picture Vitaly had shown me a few nights ago.

The man's blood had tested as clean, not the purest perhaps, but it would do. He had donated it all. He didn't have a choice. The second man had not been clean and was unsuitable. Vitaly and Fyodor had disposed of him elsewhere.

I carefully poured out a quarter of a cup, re-stoppered the bag and hung it back in the cabinet. Then I went over to Ben and looked down into his eyes. They were still heavily bloodshot but were clearing. He blinked a couple of times and stared back at me.

I told him to open his mouth. He did, and I removed his bloodied mouth guard. It had been partially bitten through. He had strong jaws.

"How do you feel?" I asked.

"Thirsty," he whispered.

I offered the cup and dribbled some blood into his mouth. He drank it cautiously, coughed, then licked his lips clean.

"More," he rasped.

"Not too much. Not yet," I told him.

"More!" His cracked voice became insistent.

I shook my head. "Feel anything else, besides thirsty?"

His brow furrowed as he gave it some thought. "Strange. Different." He spoke quietly, still feeling the effects from all that screaming. "Hollow," he added, trying to work out what had been done to him and who he was now.

"Tell me your name."

His answer was not immediate. It was as if he had to recall the information. "Bernando Idini."

"Who am I?"

"You are Leofric Pajari." He blinked a couple of times, gathering thoughts. "You have done something to me. Something that hurt." There was no accusation in his voice, it was just a statement of fact.

His eyes remained bloodshot, but were now no worse than if he'd been drinking heavily the night before. He was still pale, a grey pallor underneath his tan.

"What do you remember about a girl called Denia?"

"Denia?" I could almost see the information being dredged from memories. "Yes, I remember a Denia. Pretty girl. Her laugh... I..." he tailed off. It seemed he was trying to work something out or understand some concept that was alien to him.

"Lie still," I told him. "Ten more minutes." Ben said nothing and closed his eyes. I turned away and saw Vitaly was looking at me questioningly.

"It is okay?" he asked. I told him it was. "Will we need Fyodor? Just in case?"

"No. In fact, it would be best for you to leave. Lock the door behind you. I will call when it is safe to be unlocked again."

Even though Ben was in a weakened state I knew he would still be dangerous but unless he was immensely lucky there was no way he could overpower or harm me. Vitaly was a different matter and I did not want to lose such a dependable ally.

Vitaly nodded and left the room. I heard the heavy locks slide into place on the far side of the door.

I went over to the table where the girl, Denia, was secured. She looked asleep but I could tell she had fainted and was unconscious. The persistent horror of Ben's screaming had made her wet herself and pass out from sheer terror. I woke her up. Traditional smelling salts and pinching a tender part of the body worked.

Her eyes went wide with fear and for a moment I thought she would pass out again. I gave her my most comforting smile and tried to reassure her, telling her that it was okay - which it was as far as I was concerned - and that Ben would be with her soon - which was also true.

I returned to Ben and loosened the restraints around his head. His eyes were open and he followed what I was doing. They were no longer bloodshot and now shone with an eager feral intensity.

"Angry?" I asked as I released the straps around his legs. He said nothing. I moved on to his arms and then undid the restraints around his torso. He was free to move but remained lying there, watching me.

"What did you do to me?" Ben's voice had almost returned to normal. He sounded a little weak, but there was no hoarseness when he spoke.

"Sit up," I told him. He swung his legs over the side of the table and remained sitting there naked, looking at me with an eerie curiosity.

I told him exactly what I had done, why I had done it and what it meant for him. From the other table Denia moaned against her gag a couple of times. I remembered Ben had told me she could understand some Italian and I wondered if she believed what she was hearing. Ben glanced over then ignored her, instead listening quietly to what I was saying and taking it all in. When I finished he nodded, understanding.

"And you will teach me?" he asked.

"It is not an easy path but I will. It is why I chose you."

He slid off the metal table cautiously, taking his weight on legs that were not as shaky as he expected. "So what's the first lesson?"

"Feeding. The old fashioned way." I turned to look at the table with the girl. Ben followed my gaze.

"Denia?" he said, concern colouring his voice. I felt a jab of worry. Had I allowed enough time for the change to take him?

He went over to her, his bare feet silent on the tiled floor, and gently removed her gag. She immediately started jabbering questions at him but he hushed her. "Be still." He undid the straps securing her to the table.

I knew she would try to leap off as soon as she could, but also knew that after having been restrained for so long her body would not be as willing as her mind thought it was. I was correct.

Denia swung herself off the table towards Ben and nearly crumpled onto the tiled floor. He caught her and held her, from the pained look on her face rather more tightly than she expected. She gasped and pushed away from him. He let her go and looked back at me, expecting guidance as she staggered away around the far side of the table.

"Step one," I said to Ben, "Immobilise."

I moved fast, I was next to the girl and broke her ankle with a hard kick before either of them realised it. It also demonstrated to Ben the speed he could be capable of one day. A useful lesson.

Denia screamed, collapsing to the floor. I grabbed her arm and hauled her into a better position.

"Two - feed quickly." I jabbed two fingers at the side of her neck, my nails made small half-moon puncture marks in her dusky skin that oozed blood. "Come," I urged my new disciple. "Take her. Bite here. Drink."

He was on her quickly, biting deep into the soft flesh of her neck. She flailed against him but he wrapped his arms around her, pinning her roughly and brutally hard. I heard her ribs crack as he fed, soft slurping sounds betraying his deep thirst and his erection a sure sign of the pleasure of the feed he was experiencing.

I looked on, enjoying the spectacle the same way a father would seeing his son ride a bicycle unaided for the first time. I caught the girl staring at me and met her gaze. I think her look was meant to shame me, or show her hatred of me. All I got was a frisson of delight as her eyes lost focus and life ebbed away.

"Enough." I ordered Ben, shaking his shoulder. "Never go all the way to the end."

Reluctantly he released the girl. Her dying body dropped and her head cracked onto the hard tiles. Ben looked at me. Gore drenched his face and chest. He did not look pale anymore, in fact he looked flushed and excited.

I smiled back at him. I had resisted creating such progeny for the last forty years and now couldn't recall why I had left it so long.

"Let's get you cleaned up and dressed." I gestured to the wall. There were six photographs of men stuck there, two already with crosses through them. "Then we'll go hunting."

My disciple smiled and the dark voices inside me rejoiced.

The End

Return of the Ripper
By
John Lovell

Chapter 1

She tried to scream, but nothing came.

She could taste the salty sweetness of her blood as it filled her mouth. She was choking, no drowning in the warm sticky substance, trying desperately to clear her throat of it.

The knife had been sharp, and the cut deep. Despairingly she grappled with her assailant, aimlessly mauling his coat, desperate to be free of his grip. The frantic exertions sucking away what little breath remained. Deep down she already knew it to be a futile struggle, oxygen deprivation robbing her of the strength needed to repel this attacker. She was losing consciousness at the hand of this stranger and soon it would be over. Hands, were they really hands?

*****

"It's a bloody mess in there," said the D.S. reporting back to the car where D.I. Merton was sitting inside. "She's been hacked to pieces, just like all the others."

"So that's five now, all related I bet," Merton replied stepping out of the car.

Walking briskly across the road to the run down tenement with D.S. Jones traipsing beside him like an overexcited puppy, they entered the building.

Merton already knew this case would be unlike any other he had been involved with in his time with the Metropolitan Police Force. In twenty years, he had seen many crimes, many dead bodies, but nothing like the scene that lay before him.

In Merton's mind, the room, lit by a solitary bedside lamp, had taken on the appearance of an abattoir. On the bed lay the remains of the butchered animal that had once been Rebecca Grimes - a well know local prostitute and drug user. Adding to the illusion, the Scene of Crime Officers, in their white anti-contamination suits, busied themselves about the body collecting and bagging up the evidence.

Frank Merton was no prude. Just like his father before him, he knew what went on in these back street tenements. Merton had become a policeman out of tradition. His father and grandfather had patrolled these very streets in the heydays of the London gangs and IRA bombers. The slums had not changed, only the criminals. Back then crimes like this had a motive, but there would never have been such barbarism as this inflicted upon a woman.

*****

"What is it about Whitechapel, Frank? There can't be any connection can there, not after all this time, surely?"

Frank shrugged his shoulders, just as he always did when a superior confronted him with rhetorical questions he was unable to answer.

"Don't think there can be, Sir, not after a hundred odd years."

"A copycat then," continued Superintendent Dawes.

"Yes Sir, that would seem the most probable." Uncertain that his answer was sufficient, D.I. Frank Merton quickly added, "I'm going to dig out the old case files from back then, just to familiarise myself with the Ripper murders, it might turn up something. At least it will help me get into the mind of this sicko…"

Out of the corner of his eye, Merton could see his sergeant returning from the canteen, and an opportunity to escape this one-sided interrogation. "…But now I'm off to see the pathologist," he said, rising quickly from his chair and collecting his coat off the dilapidated mock Victorian wooden hat stand occupying one corner of the office, whilst beckoning to his D.S. who had, at that very same moment, sat down and started to unwrap a sandwich. "Jones, don't just sit there, make yourself useful - get the damn car!"

*****

"Sorry Sir," said the apologetic records clerk on the other end of Merton's smartphone, "marked for the eyes of the Home Secretary and the Police Commissioner only." It came as quite a disappointment to Merton to learn that after all this time the Ripper case files were still being kept under lock and key, and would not be released to him. Feeling frustrated, he turned to the internet browser on his phone for inspiration. Here at least, there was something he could do 'en-route' to the pathology lab.

After ten minutes of reading about Jack the Ripper and scribbling a few notes in his pocket book, Merton, still grappling for answers to questions he could not yet formalise, half turned to his driver. "Why Whitechapel Jones, and why now?" Jones, choosing to remain diplomatically silent, persevered with the task of negotiating the car through the London traffic around Hammersmith.

Merton knew that he had to get a look at those files. He knew they had been reopened not so long back to add in some new DNA evidence - and then they had been reclassified. 'A mystery within a mystery to solve another day,' he thought.

"Trains, Guv!"

"What Jones?"

"Trains Guv, Whitechapel - has good train links. Makes it easy to get in and out, if you get my drift," continued the D.S., "It's my hobby see, and Whitechapel station opened in 1876."

"It may well have done, Jones, but that doesn't explain why it is happening again or how that is even connected. It's similar - but not identical."

Opening up his notebook Merton turned to the hastily scribbled notes. Now on a mission to enlighten his sergeant with the scraps of information he had obtained earlier, he continued.

"Back then, the Ripper case file was focused on what became known as the canonical five, rather than the eleven reported murders in the borough of Whitechapel during the same period, because these had marked similarities according to Sir Melville Macnaghten. There had always been a discussion on whether it was actually six. Now I don't believe we are looking for a suspect who is trying to exactly recreate the Ripper's murders in every detail, it's more 'in the style of'. So Jones, if it is a copycat killer, we have to assume that he knows as much as we do from the information available in the public domain. Therefore, we have to know what he knows. And the first thing we need to know is how many murders to expect!"

As the car crawled through the lunchtime traffic Merton took out his smartphone once again and engrossed himself in it, searching for information that might help him, most of which was turning out to be overtly sensationalist and superficial.

Mary Nichols, murdered 31/8/1888; cause of death: a bleed out due to a cut to the throat and disemboweling.

Next, Anne Chapman, murdered 8/9/1888; cause of death: a cut to the throat and other mutilation including the removal of her womb. In this case there was at least some scant forensic evidence – a testimony by a Dr. Bagster Phillips, '.... the throat was dissevered deeply so that the incisions through the skin were jagged and reached right round the neck...'

Elizabeth Stride, the third victim, murdered 30/09/1888; cause of death: a deep laceration across the throat. This case was more interesting to Merton because in a statement by a Mr. Israel Schwartz, it suggested there was an accomplice, or mastermind.

The fourth victim Catherine Eddows, murdered 30/09/1888; cause of death: loss of blood due to dissection. Beside the now ritual slaughter, there was massive disfigurement too and again, a kidney and womb had been removed. This was of interest to Merton, he was unsure as to why, but it was.

The last of the canonical five to be murdered was Mary Kelly, murdered 9/11/1888. This was by far the most gruesome crime. She was found virtually skinned to the bone. She had been discovered in bed next to a bedside table piled high with human flesh, her cadaver hardly recognisable as human anymore.

Unaware that they were approaching the morgue, Merton had one last thought: there were five, but what if Elizabeth Stride's murder had been interrupted? Would that mean that there should only have been four? After all he was investigating more murders than that many now. Or, should the murder of Martha Tabram be added to the list? She was murdered on 7/8/1888 and there was enough circumstantial evidence, including mutilation, to include her.

Satisfied there were five, Merton got out of the car, but still the voice in his head would not go away. 'Five, why only five, the police had no leads, so why did it stop?' Merton knew only too well that serial killers who revel in the gratification of their crimes do not stop, they get caught. In his heart Merton hoped he was wrong. If five was the number, then they were too late. There would be no more killings.

Chapter 2

"Darnley, Forensic Pathologist." Gloved hand extended, Merton shook it cautiously. "An interesting case we have here. In fact, very interesting." Darnley continued after pausing to open the examination room door and lead the inspector and his sergeant into the brightly lit white tiled room. There in front of them on the post mortem table lay the body of the latest victim of the 'Copycat Ripper.' A title Merton had decided to pin on his 'as yet unknown assailant.'

Darnley pulled back the sheet to reveal a ghostly white cadaver; chalk-like in appearance by the migration of what little blood remained into the large purple bruises coalesced around her buttocks where they made contact with the stainless steel table. Looking at the body it reminded Merton of a white plimsoll, the laces replaced by sutures to keep the gash from the sternum to the pelvic floor closed.

"For once your killer may have slipped up," said Darnley turning back to face Merton. "Did you know all the victims were pregnant?"

"I do now," said Merton, trying hard not to sound surprised and wondering why this fact had not been disclosed before.

"Ah yes, well, we have only just by chance discovered it ourselves. As you already know, in the other four murders the womb was also completely removed. However, this lady was having an ectopic pregnancy, and therefore the embryo was developing outside of the womb." Darnley paused momentarily, to study the Inspector's face for a sign of acknowledgement. "So we ran further blood tests on the other victims – all of them were pregnant too. A stroke of luck really, seeing how you hadn't yet given us permission to release them to their families for disposal."

"Something else too," continued the pathologist. "Although most of the mutilations are crude, including the removal of the other organs. The removal of the womb on all the victims has been done with exacting precision. It's almost like the killer used a laser scalpel."

Merton's mind was racing, the voices in his head debating the scene that lay before him. 'Why would someone want to extract intact wombs with embryos in them so precisely and yet inflict so much unnecessary butchering? Was it to try and hide the removal of the womb? It hadn't worked in 1888, the medical records of the victims had proved that. Back then though, forensic science would not have noticed any discernible differences in the methods of removal – even if there had been any.' Try as he might Merton found himself unwittingly making comparisons to the original Victorian murders, rather than focusing on the present. Once again he reprimanded his inner-self. 'These murders are different, and so is the killer.'

'No,' thought Merton, returning to the present, 'to cover up the method used to remove the womb – maybe that was it.'

"Thank you Darnley, very interesting. Have you formed any ideas as to why these wombs were removed so precisely?"

"Well, that's your department. All I can say is that an embryo removed at this period of gestation," said Darnley pointing to the pink perfectly formed embryo in a kidney dish, "could be viable for only a minute or two in a separated womb before oxygen starvation kicked in."

"Anything else of note from the forensic evidence, Darnley, I should be made aware of?" Merton made sure he stressed the words 'should' and 'made' as much as possible. Merton duly noted that Darnley hesitated before answering.

"We believe we found some traces of skin from under the nails of the victim, but have been unable to match it to anything on our database. So we don't actually know what it is."

*****

Back in the car it became apparent to Merton, that if the killer was still in the mood to commit more crimes, he would have to get the area around Whitechapel put under surveillance. 'But where?' Deciding he needed to understand the killer's movements better, he would map out the murder sites and possible escape routes as soon as he got back to the station. That would be a good starting point he mused. Worryingly, in the back of his mind there was a nagging doubt he had missed something, a thought that would not go away, but, was also failing to render itself into language and reveal its secret.

"Lunchtime, Guv," D.S. Jones piped up, spotting a chippy on the street corner, "I could murder a Steak & Kidney pie and chips."

"That's it Jones." Merton was no longer searching his mind for the answer, it was now blindingly obvious. "Well done."

"Who me Guv?"

"Yes, you have unwittingly come up with a revelation...a revelation!"

"I have?" replied the bewildered sergeant.

"In all the cases, old and new, none of the removed organs have ever been found."

We can conclude then, that they were needed in some way, maybe as a trophy, or for some medical purpose. But the way they organs were removed, one carefully, and one crudely, beggars the question; why differentiate? In 1888 no one would have noticed the difference - if there was any difference to notice of course. But, the more I think about it, the more I am certain: the butchery in these copycats is a crude attempt to cover up the taking of the womb. So why take the kidneys and the livers also? Obviously to make us think it is a 'Jack the Ripper' copycat and to throw us off the scent and lead us down the proverbial garden path. But this could also be the killer's undoing - trying to maintain a deception gives us a chance to catch him."

"Come on let's get back to the station. We have a profile to build, and I need to get a look at the original case file…. somehow!"

Jones giving up on a chance to reply, or any lunch, started the car heading back towards SW1.

Chapter 3

"Frank, do you really need me to put a submission in to get a look at these case files?" enquired Superintendent Dawes, his large frame hovering over Merton as he sat at his desk, like a hawk stalking a mouse.

"Yes, Sir, if you wouldn't mind."

"Well then, it's just as well I already had," said Dawes pointing to the locked evidence box in the corner of the room. Handing Merton the key, he continued, "I'm under strict orders that no one other than yourself and your sergeant can see them."

Dawes turned to walk away and as he did so Merton was sure he heard the chief mutter under his breath, "bloody bureaucrats."

The metal evidence box was as dusty as time itself, but nothing compared to the contents. Brown folders full of painstakingly written testimonies, all in longhand, written in an age when ink and nib was king.

Merton compared each document to what he had discovered already and started to map out a profile of each case, including the exact location of the murder. There was much more here than he had expected, but still very little existed in the way of post-mortem details. He knew it would be that way, forensic science was still in its infancy back then. Eventually he found what he had wanted most to see. The folder containing the forensic evidence from the re-examination of a shawl carried out in 2005, before it was bought at auction in 2007 and well before The Mail reported that the murderer had been uncovered - namely one of the original suspects: A Polish hairdresser. But the documents in the folder did not support this revelation or identify the murderer. Merton found himself wondering if it was even the same shawl or whether the evidence had been deliberately tampered with in some way. For there in front of him, he saw a sentence that made the hairs on the back of his neck stand to attention, it simply stated, 'BLOOD OF UNKNOWN ORIGIN AND TYPE.'

Confused, Merton put down the file, unsure that it was even relevant to his case. Darnley had said the skin sample was unidentifiable too. He had to stay focused. He was looking for a copycat killer, not 'Jack the Ripper.'

At that moment Jones entered the room with more food and coffee. "Bloody hell, you've been busy Guv." Examining a large pin board that seemed to engulf the room his eyes were immediately drawn to the street map Merton had found in the time capsule that was the evidence box. "Look how the spread of murders to the north of the underground are focused, Guv, not on Whitechapel station as you would think, but on a station farther up the line, Aldgate East." Eager to impress with his knowledge of the history of the London Underground, Jones continued. "Did you know they moved it? They closed St Mary's and moved Aldgate East - well east." Tracing back the route on the map, Jones continued. "Part of the old site is still there behind an electronic hoarding – might be worth taking a look, if only to rule out the fact that the killer is not disposing vital evidence there."

With nothing better to do Merton reluctantly agreed. "Let's do it tomorrow. Come prepared - bring torches."

Chapter 4

It was not without some trepidation that Merton approached the large advertising hoarding on Whitechapel High Street. There was scant enough evidence to follow up on and this had the feeling of a being another dead end. Turning his car into Goulston Street he was pleased to see the Fast Food Bar open, even though today was not the day for the world famous Petticoat Lane market. D.I. Jones was already there with what looked like a coffee on the counter waiting for him.

"Well Jones, what do you reckon? Is this going to be another wild goose chase?"

Having already surveyed the site through the railings, Jones was eager to report back his findings. "If you go and look through the railings over there, Sir," said the D.S. pointing to the spot, "you can see the door that leads down to the tunnels. The site was never completely filled in as it makes a good access point for the engineers when they need to get down to the tracks. However, getting in may be a problem as there is only one set of gates I can see, and they are locked."

Merton smiled. "A criminal needs no key, Jones, but I have one. Very obliging are the London Transport Police, they sent one over to the office."

*****

Invigorated by coffee and the bacon sandwich that followed, they made their way through the zinc coated metal gate and down onto a severely overgrown path, discernible only from the undergrowth surrounding it by the outline of the badly rusted handrail that ran alongside. Carefully they made their way over to the small brick protrusion standing at the end of the path and the rusty metal door built into it. In Jones's mind, it reminded him of an outdoor toilet, but he opted to keep that observation to himself.

Merton was first to notice the absence of the padlock on the hasp and staple that should have secured the door. Surveying the area immediately to the right of the outbuilding, Jones quickly located it. "Here it is," he said whilst trying to disentangle himself from a particular nasty bramble. "Now there's a thing, it's been cut through."

"Okay so let's be careful then from here on in," said Merton, beginning to revaluate the folly of coming here. Maybe there was a connection here after all.

Despite its age and the condition of the rusty hinges, the door opened easily enough. Immediately the pair found themselves in a tile-lined stairwell, lit only by the dappled sunlight crossing the threshold of the doorway. Switching on their torches, like two intrepid explorers, they made their way down the spiral staircase they found inside.

"It's not far down to the tracks. This line is only just below ground," whispered Jones, who, for some reason, had decided this was not the time to speak at his normal rumbustious volume.

On reaching the bottom of the stairs, a second door led them out onto the old disused platform. In the distance, they could just discern a faint glow from the direction of Whitechapel station, half a mile away, where the trains emerged from the inky blackness surrounding them out into the daylight.

"There should be another passage along here somewhere to get us onto the District Line," said Jones, stepping forward to take up the lead position as he and Merton continued along the platform, "and don't forget

Guv, although this may be a disused station, it is not a disused line."

No sooner had Jones finished forewarning his superior, as if to command, the tunnel started to lighten and the unmistakable squeal of an approaching train coming around a bend reached their ears. A few seconds later the train appeared, its headlights lighting up the tunnel, and then Merton saw it, "look over there" he exclaimed. "There is somebody else down here with us."

For a brief moment Merton thought he had seen someone standing in an alcove cut into the other side of the tunnel wall. Patiently waiting for the train to pass, he looked again, but the figure had disappeared. "We need to cross the line, Jones."

"Oh very well, now," Jones replied, momentarily slipping into the dialect of his forefathers, exposing his Welsh upbringing. "Just don't touch the rails, see, especially that one there. It's got enough juice passing through it to vaporise a tunnel rat."

Frustratingly they waited for another train to pass, and Merton could just make out, with the aid of the train's headlights, a door built into the back wall of the alcove.

Stepping carefully over the twin tracks of the Hammersmith and City Line, they made their way over to the alcove.

The heavy metal door, to Merton's surprise, swung open easily enough. Behind it lay another tunnel, its smooth matt concrete walls sucking up all the light their torches could deliver. Stepping through the door they continued along its gently descending path, the echo of every step being amplified around them as the sound bounced off the walls.

No sooner had they got used to the crammed conditions of the concrete pipe they found themselves in - it stopped, only to be replaced by a rough-cut tunnel hewn out of the bedrock.

"What do you make of this then, Jones?"

"Well, it could be part of an old water drainage course. There's a subterranean river close by running under the Tower of London and into the Thames. It's one of the reasons they built the Tower where they did – it sits on a natural sewer you might say."

With Jones taking up the lead position once again, they continued on down. Merton had always considered him to be the most valuable member of his small team of detectives, and he was proving it once again. Whenever there was a difficult decision to be made, Jones would be the one person he could turn to. Uncannily his hunches often turned out to be correct and Merton was warming to the idea that this 'wild goose chase' might actually produce some results.

With only the light from their torches to guide them, they continued down the dark, dank, musty tunnel which had now become quite slippery underfoot and Merton was sure he could now hear the sound of running water reverberating off the craggy walls from somewhere below.

Eventually the tunnel flattened out from its slippery descent, opening up into a huge void, swallowing what little light their torches could produce to illuminate it. When their eyes had adjusted to the blackness, they could see that they had emerged into in a large vaulted chamber. To Merton it seemed like he was standing in the middle of some underground cathedral, or maybe more accurately, he thought, a crypt. As the light from their torches danced along the walls opposite, they could trace the outline of the ancient bricks rising majestically out of the water to form arches that held up a brick ceiling, ten metres above their heads.

"Now just look at that," Jones whispered under his breath, "it's like being in some sort of subterranean dungeon," Merton hoped that Jones's hunch was wrong this time. "We must be directly underneath the Tower of London. Look-see, there's a doorway over there. I wonder if this was part of an old escape route built from the tower to get the king to safety."

Making their way carefully along an ancient brick built jetty, they approached the door. Merton was sure he could hear a low-pitched hum coming from inside - the type of sound electrical equipment made. Merton instinctively reached out and grabbed his sergeant's arm, and raising a finger to his mouth signalled him to be silent.

Like two cats on a hunt, they proceeded judiciously through the doorway.

Chapter 5

On the other side of the doorway, the detectives were greeted by a vast array of scientific paraphernalia stretching out in front of them. And the chamber, hacked out of the very bedrock the Tower of London was built on, was being illuminated by an eerie blue light making it all the harder to discern anything in detail.

At the far end of the room, Merton could barely make out the dark shadowy figure hunched over a particular advanced looking piece of electronic apparatus.

Before Merton could comprehend the scene before him, the figure turned and he felt his heart skip a beat. Blind panic overawing his senses. In front of him stood a man, like no man he had ever seen before. This was no ordinary criminal; this was hardly even a man in any sense of the word as he understood it.

"So you have found my humble abode," rasped the tall pale figure.

Even in the subdued blue light, Merton could distinguish the almost translucent, ghostly white, appearance of the suspect. All except for the eyes, for they looked strangely un-human.

Struggling to regain his composure, Merton tried to sound authoritative. "We're here investigating the murders in Whitechapel." How hollow those words now sounded to him.

"Ah," rasped the figure again. "You have learnt much since the last time I was here."

Merton's mind started reeling. 'Last time….'

"So you admit it then, you are Jack the Ripper?" Merton asked, almost refusing to believe the words as he spoke them.

"Yes, I suppose I am," replied the figure.

Unseen by the stranger, Jones had made his way round the jagged stone buttresses that formed part of the walls of the room. From his position behind one of the humming consoles, he could wait for his chance to take the stranger down. Summoning upon all the strength his legs could muster he leapt out at the figure, but not quickly enough to stop the stranger turning to face him.

The stranger, with a single motion of his arm traced out a semi-circle of pure blue blinding light, radiating out from the pencil-like device he held in his hand. The blue laser light slicing through Jones's spinal column leaving his head attached to his torso by a flap of skin at the back of his neck.

By the time Jones's knees made contact with the floor, he was already dead. Falling forwards, like an overturned ketchup bottle, D.S. Jones's life-force ebbed away, his blood taking on a black hue in the eerie blue light as it spread out, stopping only momentarily to fill the small depressions in the stone as it snaked its way across the floor.

"Now, are you going to try anything stupid?" Rasped the figure in a voice Merton had never heard the like of before.

"No, you have the better of me at the moment," said Merton, trying to conceal his fear and grief for his fallen comrade.

"But why, and how? Jack? Is that really your name even?"

A wry smile passed fleetingly across the stranger's face, and for all the world, Merton could not place a man with features so different to his idea of what a serial killer should look like. The stranger stepped forward into a puddle of light and Merton saw that his skin was even paler than he had first thought, and his eyes were definitely pink with dark red pupils. Merton assumed the stranger must be an Albino, even though he had never actually met one before.

"I suppose you would like an explanation?" the stranger enquired.

"Well yes of course, and what do you mean about the last time?" enquired Merton. "Oh and your real name of course because we both know it's not Jack, don't we?"

The stranger suppressed the laugh that rose within from the notion he was being interrogated. "My name is Ze'Crath, and yes I was the one you called Jack the Ripper, so many of your years ago. I am an Alburian."

For a moment, Merton had a fancy he was talking to a vampire from some small Eastern European country nobody would quite know where to locate on an atlas.

"An Alburian, you say?"

"Yes, from the planet Alburia circling a star you know by the name of Pollux, in the constellation you call Gemini. It takes nearly sixty of your years for me to get home from here, so it has been about one hundred and twenty years since I was here last. And, although we are long lived, and this is part of our disease, for the duration of the journey we travel here in suspended animation.

"Part of your disease?" blurted out Merton, unsure as to whether he was being taken for a complete idiot. Merton decided his best hope for survival was to humour him and play along with this fantasy, hoping the stranger would finally slip up and reveal his true identity. If anything, 'Merton of the Yard' was not going to fall for all this Star Trek rubbish, even if his life was in peril.

"Yes." Sensing a tone of disbelief in Merton's voice Ze'Crath continued. "You are an arrogant race. You dare to presume you have a special purpose in the universe. Well your only purpose is to furnish 'me' with what I need." To Merton the menace in his voice was now unmistakable. "We harvest from you what we need. It's not much, and you are allowed to survive and flourish on this lovely planet." Merton detected a note of irony in his voice. "You see; we are one of the oldest races in this galaxy. We visited your planet over one million years ago, like we did many others that suited our purpose. We searched for many years to find planets exactly like Alburia, because we knew life would evolve here along similar lines to our own. We came to your planet with a single objective – to splice our DNA into the primitive humans that existed here at the time so they would be a compatible match for us in the future when we needed them. We stayed around just long enough for the modern human species to develop, returning on occasions, just to check on how you were progressing." Ze'Crath paused for a moment. "Ah yes, those were the days when my forbears were treated like gods and offered sacrifices for us to feast upon."

"But why go to all that trouble?" Merton was still unsure if he was being told anything but a fanciful story.

"We knew a time would come when our DNA would start to degrade. Too many generations, too many diseases - they have enfeebled us. So we come to your world to take what we need, what we planted you might say. I see your planet too is now starting to face the same issues we did. Drug resistance, DNA mutations, ever increasing forms of crippling disease, and all the time the humblest life form on your planet, the bacterium, becomes ever stronger the more you try to kill it. It happened just the same way on our world, so we come here every now and again for a little vacation and to take back the genetic material we need to survive." Ze'Crath paused for a moment's reflection before continuing. "In your terms we are a sterile race."

Merton stiffened his resolve, "You mean the liver, kidneys and wombs you take from your victims."

"Ah," Ze'Crath laughed, "no just the wombs. Those other parts are what we consider delicacies. After all, we are on holiday."

"But I have told you enough already." Ze'Crath's tone darkened and the furrows on his brow crinkled in such a way as to resemble crepe paper. "You will make an excellent addition to my workforce, seeing how I accidentally killed the last one who disobeyed my instructions. But that will not happen again once I have fitted you with a restrainer." Suddenly a pale green light surrounded Merton and he found himself unable to move. He was passing out.

Ze'Crath smiled as he looked down upon the collapsed Merton. He was pleased. Soon this meddling fool would be helping him obtain another womb to replace the empty one he had recently returned with, and in a moment of rage - lashed out and killed his useless 'assistant'.

Chapter 6

Merton awoke in a small cell just off the main cave. A door made from iron bars, rusty with age, barred his way out onto the connecting corridor.

"Ah, you're awake then." Ze'Crath said, approaching with what looked like food. "Soon you will be working for me. You see, I need you to do certain tasks for me." Ze'Crath handed Merton the food, Merton put it down. He was not yet that hungry, or stupid enough to taste it. "You see we have a different way of inseminating our females and it is not compatible with your method. So, I need an accomplice to do it for me, an agent you might say. Just one more womb before I can leave your world." He paused, turning his back to Merton, before continuing. "I have already selected a whore with the correct DNA for you to inseminate for me. For which I will provide you with a specially modified vial of semen, and in keeping with your sexual proclivities, you insert it into her vagina where it will instantly discharge the fluid. Then when the time is right I will harvest the resultant embryo and return to Alburia."

Ze'Crath swung back around and stared menacingly at his accomplice. Merton shifted uneasily. His discomfort magnified by the cold stone floor numbing his buttocks. Ze'Crath continued, oblivious to Merton's distress. "Tonight you will work for me, and then in six weeks' time I can depart this place. If you are thinking to do otherwise, you might like to feel behind your ear. I have placed a control device there that will make you submit to my will.… or you will die."

"I suppose that is what happened to the other guy then," Merton observed. Ze'Crath bowed his head slightly in acknowledgement and left the room. 'But what will become of me after tonight?' Merton thought.

Merton spent the rest of the day contemplating what he could do to escape from his predicament. The situation looked hopeless and he was afraid. Afraid that he would never again see the daughter he loved; soon to graduate from school. Or, his wife of eighteen years - eighteen years of putting up with the unsociable hours policemen worked. How much he had taken her for granted and how little he had seen of his daughter growing up. How much he would give to be at home with them both now.

*****

In a small ground floor flat, Abigayle busied herself, getting ready for her final trick of the day. She sat in front of the mirror and applied her makeup. Not so bad, she thought as she finished off with a flick of eyeliner. The phone call she received earlier that day had been unusual in that she could not place the accent of the caller. It seemed strangely foreign, Eastern European possibly, but his use of English had been very formal and polite. She was good at her job and worth the money he was going to pay. At least she would not have to stand out in the cold tonight. The 'trick' was going to pay double for special favours, and she was desperate for the money.

The doorbell rang and Abigayle answered it as she always did, wearing a heavy dressing gown so as not to raise the suspicions of her neighbours. "Come on in luv. What would you like me to call you?" asked Abi in a loud and slow voice, noting the device behind Merton's ear and assuming incorrectly that he was hard of hearing.

Merton mumbled out his name, it was all he could manage. The pain in his head would let him say no more. How he wished he could tell her the truth of it, and tell her to run for her life, but the control device would not let him. Besides, he knew his only chance of escape would require him to comply with Ze'Crath's demands. After all, six weeks was a long time for an opportunity to arise.

Barely half-an-hour had passed before Abigayle was waving Merton off and bolting the door for the night. Outside Merton crossed the road and got into the waiting car. It disturbed Merton to see Ze'Crath sitting there in the place Jones used to inhabit.

"Well Merton, how did it go?" he asked.

Merton gave his captor a blow-by-blow account and saw that Ze'Crath seemed pleased. Maybe after all this was over he would let him go.

On returning to Ze'Crath's lair by the same route he had taken with Jones the previous day, he was surprised to find an oblong cylinder lying in the middle of the control room.

"Step in please," commanded his keeper.

Merton obliged, he had no will to do otherwise as the restrainer exacted its control over him, the throbbing in his head crawling over all his synapses. To Merton it felt like a herd of wild elephants trampling through his cranium.

Chapter 7

Merton remembered nothing when he awoke from what seemed to him like a normal night's sleep. Why was he in a cave behind bars? How did he get there? Why could he not remember anything? He had a strange notion he had been dreaming about something, something too horrible to describe. But now he was awake, the place seemed oddly familiar.

"Ah Merton, did you enjoy your little sleep?" He remembered. "Tonight is the night, we go harvesting. You have been in suspended animation for six weeks. Your disappearance was all over the news. Normally I go for people who will not be missed. It saves a lot of trouble later. Come we have work to do, and your car will be very helpful again."

*****

Abigayle already knew she was pregnant, again, and had booked an appointment to get a termination. She put it down as one of the hazards of the job, but she was normally so careful. Still it would soon be a distant memory. At least she could go to the pub tonight and drink heavily, like she always did.

The knock on the door was welcome for this would be her final trick of the night. Putting her eye to the peephole, she could see Merton standing there on the other side of the door. She slid back the bolt. To her surprise, the door swung open wildly knocking her to the ground and before she could let out any sort of sound, a scaly white hand had covered her mouth. She tried to scream but this stranger's hand was pressing down too hard on her mouth, suffocating her as he pinched her nose between his thumb and fingers. In her attacker's other hand, she could see only too clearly the large serrated edged blade being brought towards her neck.

With one quick movement, Ze'Crath sliced through her unprotected neck a cut so deep that it exposed her windpipe. Blood bubbled from the wound as she fought to get her breath. Grabbing her by the hair Ze'Crath dragged her, kicking and flailing, over to the bed and threw her onto it. Looking over his shoulder, Ze'Crath issued his instructions to Merton who was standing forlornly in the doorway. "Go, return to the car." Merton was powerless to do otherwise, the alien restrainer pulsated with every syllable Ze'Crath uttered increasing its hold on him. Dutifully he complied, every thought of escape driven from his mind by the overwhelming pain in his head.

Ze'Crath could now feast a little and get off this miserable planet. With a deft hand his next cut along the medial line from the sternum to the pelvic floor made Abigayle arch her back, the searing pain overawing her senses. As the disembowelling continued, with every cut Ze'Crath watched the white sheets turning red and Abigayle's weakening response to the new intrusion of the knife - until she twitched no more.

Like some demented gastronome, Ze'Crath feasted on her liver and delighted in the sweetness of it. So much nicer was this human meat than the artificial protein he had to endure on Alburia, he thought.

Abigayle no longer cared.

Expertly removing the womb with his laser scalpel, Ze'Crath placed it into the square metallic box he had brought. The portable stasis box would ensure the organ remained alive for thirty minutes until he could get back to his sanctuary and prepare to make ready his departure off of this primitive world.

Merton was waiting in the car, Ze'Crath joined him, "Aldgate, now," and Merton duly obliged.

Chapter 8

Back at the sanctuary, Merton sat silently in the corner of his cell. The throbbing in his head was starting to abate and he could again think more clearly. 'How can I get away?' 'Get back to safety?' 'Get back home to my wife and family?' In the darkness Merton sobbed quietly to himself, a broken man.

"Ah Merton, I see you are conscious once again. I must thank you for the excellent dinner tonight." Ze'Crath laughed. "You really were most helpful." Ze'Crath knew the restrainer had a limited life before it destroyed the wearer's mind, and Merton may yet prove useful again, should some unforeseen circumstances prevent him from leaving tonight.

Merton could at last form words in his mind and open his mouth "W…hy w…ombs?"

"Ah, the embryos, you mean," corrected Ze'Crath. "Well they are our future. You see no Alburian female has been able to conceive for 1000's of years, so we harvest embryos from compatible species we have adjusted throughout the galaxy and plant them into the wombs of specially modified surrogates back home. Each of these embryos will be held in stasis until that time and be modified to ensure it will develop into an Alburian female hybrid. These mutants are then used to restock our race until they can no longer bear any more spawnlings."

Ze'Crath paused, should he tell him the rest? Should he tell him that they were kept in conditions very similar to the farmed animals of his world? That the first generation were nothing more than baby producing machines. It was their offspring that were the real prize. Put to work they became the playthings of the Alburians. Genetically adapted they could copulate with the Alburian males, enslaved to produce the offspring his world needed. The fate of these hybrids when their fertile days were over? Or the way their genetic material was used to make drugs for the medicines the Alburians needed to reach their millennium. No he didn't have the time. He needed to make ready his departure and he had spent too much of it already talking to this underling.

Silently he continued his work - disconnecting the wombs encased in the stasis boxes from the machine providing life support, he knew that nothing must go wrong now. In thirty minutes' time he must be on-board his ship bound for Alburia.

As soon as all the stasis cases had been relayed from the cave to the jetty, he pressed a button on the small remote control he was holding. The black water in the tunnel immediately started to lighten up to a bright blue hue, as blue as the sky on a sunny day. A large metallic cylindrical object rose out of the water and sat on the surface. Ze'Crath pressed another button and an aperture opened in the wall of the cylinder into which he placed the stasis boxes. His shuttle was now ready to depart.

Ze'Crath had already sent out a signal to his star ship hidden behind the Earth's moon. Fully automatic it had responded and now approached the Earth. Soon he would be gone. Returning to the sanctuary, he had only a few more things to do before he could depart. Throwing a switch on the console in front of him, the tunnel that Merton had arrived by from the underground was sealed with a solid concrete door rising out of the floor at the point it entered the vaulted underground waterway. Now for Merton, his work here was complete. He too had to go the same way as his other agents. He knew only too well that eventually all bodies must be accounted for – such a pity because he had grown quite fond of his pet.

Returning to the jetty Ze'Crath pushed another button on the remote control. A large cage at the end of the jetty rose up out of the water. Ze'Crath walked over to the partly submerged lock-up, opened the door and made sure the time-lock device was functioning correctly.

Merton could feel the restrainer starting to pulse again.

In the corner of the room Ze'Crath dragged a heavy sack out of one of the stasis chambers and out onto the jetty. From within his cell, Merton could just make out the faint sound of the splash as Ze'Crath tipped Jones's body out of the sack and into the partially submerged cage.

Returning to Merton's cell Ze'Crath opened the door. The restrainer pulsed once more and Merton involuntarily found himself outside on the jetty, staring into the cage where Jones's body lay in the water. "Get in."

Try as he might he could not resist the pull of the restrainer, involuntarily Merton obeyed. Ze'Crath pressed another button on the remote and the restrainer fell off Merton's head and through the bars that formed the floor of the cage. But it was too late, before Merton's mind had cleared sufficiently to realise his life was in peril, the cage door closed and the time-lock engaged.

"Two months should be long enough in the water I think, before you are found floating in the Thames," tormented Merton's captor as he pushed another button on his remote. The cage lurched and then started its slow descent back into the underground river.

Merton realised his time was up. Frantically he tried to open the cage door, but the lock had no visible way of being removed that he could see. He could detect no weakness in the iron bars either as he desperately tugged on them to try and loosen them. As the water slowly engulfed him all sense of hope evaporated. He felt as though his lungs were about to burst as he tried desperately to cling to life, but he was starting to lose consciousness through asphyxiation. As the light played on the surface of the water, Merton was sure he could make out the faces of his wife and daughter dancing in the ripples. Reaching out he tried to touch them one last time as his battle for survival came to an end.

Three a.m. and Ze'Crath was ready to board his shuttle. He pressed the final button on his remote control and a wall of rock started to rise out of the floor in the entrance to his sanctum, hiding it until it would be needed again.

Settling himself in behind the shuttle's controls, Ze'Crath pushed a few buttons on the panel in front of him. Silently, the shuttle moved off over the water and out into the Thames. Ze'Crath engaged the camouflage circuit and the shuttle all but disappeared against the background as it moved out under Tower Bridge and into the centre of the Thames, steadily picking up speed as it did so.

With barely a ripple, it rose from the water, up into the sky, and was gone.

Ze'Crath was pleased his mission had gone so smoothly. Soon, he would be on board his star ship for the journey home to Pollux and his beloved Alburia. Even at half-light speed, it would take sixty Earth years to get there.

He wondered if his partner had missed him, and thought of how grown up his spawnling, Sug'dh'Hen, would be by the time he arrived back. How he hated these long voyages, the time spent in stasis, but he knew it was the only way; to go any faster on these long journeys would be disastrous. The space-time dilation factor would be too great, and he would return too far into Alburia's future. He checked the computer '0.5C'. Space-time dilation factor: 1.154. Not too bad he thought, not even a hundred Alburian largs would have passed since he left. It was nothing for a species that lived for a thousand largs, but this would be his last trip, he was no longer the young Alburian that trained for deep space missions nigh on 400 largs ago.

He checked on his cargo and found to his satisfaction, each stasis box humming away quietly as if singing a lullaby to its precious contents. He checked the names on each of the boxes against his manifest: Marcy, Lucy, Chloe, Rebecca and Abigayle.

Rendezvousing with his star ship, Ze'Crath manoeuvred the shuttle into the hold. Quickly transferring the cargo to the stasis chambers. Ze'Crath made his way up to the bridge and punched the coordinates for home and Jack the Ripper was gone for another hundred and twenty years.

Chapter 9

The twin moons rose over Alburia, and Chloe looked out from her small room up at them. She imagined her mother to be up there, free, playing amongst the stars. It was not the name given to her by her captors, for she had no name. It had been her grandmother's name. She remembered very little of her mother, a first generation hybrid, other than the tattoo she had branded onto her forehead. Chloe had never forgotten what her mother had once said - the tattoo was the name of her 'Earth' mother, all the hybrids had one.

Chloe had been removed from the breeding farm at an early age. Her ten sisters had already gone and she would be the last. Her mother, no longer able to breed, would be euthanized. Chloe had seen this for herself, but did not understand its true purpose. All she knew was being euthanized was the end.

She had seen Abigayle euthanized. She could still remember the screams of Aunty Abi as she was lowered into the large glass cylinder, only to be moments later minced up by the rotating blades spinning mercilessly at the bottom of the tube tearing and eviscerating her flesh. With every rotation, Abi became slowly engulfed in her own pulp as it rose up the glass, until nothing else remained. She remembered how red it was, and seeing it draining away through an outlet valve and into a pipe that disappeared out of the building.

Chloe had no idea where it led or for what reason. She hoped it was for some higher purpose and Abi had gone on to a place of freedom. The very word freedom was considered blasphemous. Even thinking about it could get her into trouble. But no, the restrainer behind her ear remained silent.

The memories of her upbringing started to flood back and invade her consciousness. How she loathed those years - treated like caged animals, worse than the pets the Alburians kept with them when they came to visit, pointing and prodding her, or one of her sisters. She did not understand what it was at that time to be branded, the inside of her left arm bore the letters Zart-E1297-C-10, her right arm: Sug'dh'Hen.

So Chloe had decided that she would take her grandmother's name. It would be her name and only she would know it. It was the only thing she could possess that could not be taken from her, and one day maybe, she too would travel amongst the stars and see the Earth for herself.

*****

Sug'dh'Hen was busying himself for the arrival of his father. He knew all too well he would be disappointed, for his hybrid had not yet conceived.

Dinner would be difficult - every hybrid had a unique reference that could trace back their lineage to the planet of origin. His: Zart-E1297-C-10, would reflect badly on his father if she did not conceive soon, seeing how it was bred from one of the hybrids he had brought back from Earth fifty largs ago. And, with his father being an influential member on the board of the science faculty on Alburia – the news would be not be welcome at all.

Presently the hover-ride pulled up outside. Sug'dh'Hen's 'verdoom' opened the door to greet her partner's birth father.

Chloe busied herself preparing the table as the food dispenser hummed away in the corner preparing the protein supplements into an almost edible form. How she hated the fact that this food was artificially enhanced to impart some flavour, unlike the bland, basic, supplements she was always given.

Dinner proceeded in almost silence as Chloe waited table. Ze'Crath, having surveyed the hybrid with displeasure throughout most of the meal was the first to speak. "So, why has this 'Zart' not yet given you an heir?"

Sug'dh'Hen tried to explain it was not through the lack of trying. "Maybe the sickness is accelerating. Maybe sterility is starting to affect second gens now?"

"Maybe," replied Ze'Crath. "In which case we would have had a better meal on her liver than this muck you serve."

Chloe flinched as Ze'Crath rose from the table and pressed the point of a knife into her belly and violently pushing her away so she fell to the ground. Ze'Crath turned around to his spawnling and continued. "In that case we had better send her away to the faculty for some tests, or maybe we just send her to the recycler anyway."

Ze'Crath did not see Chloe bang her head on the side of the table as she fell severely enough to dislodge the restrainer. Chloe rubbed the side of her head and the puncture wound where the restrainer had been, and felt the trickle of blood running down her cheek. With every passing moment, an increased sense of awareness swept over her - and what she was.

'Recycler….Recycler, that is where they sent Aunt Abi!' the words reverberating around in Chloe's mind to the exclusion of everything else. Chloe was now experiencing a new sensation - that of terror.

Taking a large knife from the serving table to her right, she thrust the blade as hard as she could into Ze'Crath's back.

Yelling out in pain, he slumped to the floor. Wasting no time in the confusion it created. Chloe ran to the door. This was her chance to escape.

Running out into the hover way, she disappeared into the night.

*****

Chloe only stopped running when she got to the limit of the great metropolis. When she had been a breedling, in the care of her mother, she had heard talk amongst the other hybrids that some others, like her, had escaped and were free – and she desperately wanted to be free. The recycler would not be her fate.

That night Chloe swore an oath to herself: One day she would be free. One day she would set all the hybrids like herself free, and one day, she would return to her ancestral home - 'Earth.'

The End

About the Authors
Carla Kovach
Carla is a playwright, screenplay writer and author from Redditch in Worcestershire. Other works include novels Flame, To Let, Whispers Beneath the Pines and Meet Me at Marmaris Castle.

Vanessa Morgan
Vanessa has written articles for many genealogical magazines. Other published works include 'Worcestershire, a Family History Guidebook' for The History Press. She has also written a 'Murder and Crime' series for The History Press. With the hundred year anniversary of WW1, she began producing a series of books based on a magazine published at the time called 'The War Illustrated – 1914-15.' 'The First Year,' and, '1915-16, The Second Year,' are both available on Amazon.

Vanessa has been dabbling in fiction for some time and as her interests lie in murder and crime (the bloodier the better), she is excited to be a writer for the Dyzturbya horror series.

Brooke Venables
Brooke is delighted to be working alongside a group of talented writers and publishing her debut short story for the Dyzturbya collection. Brooke caught the creative writing bug as part of her studies for a degree in

humanities. She has plenty of ideas in the pipeline for future publications so watch this space.

Mark Wallace

Although this is not Mark Wallace's first work of fiction, it is the first published under his real name as his action thrillers are written under a pseudonym, though you will find his amusing and factual account of a trip of a lifetime to New Zealand under his real name also on Amazon kindle. But let's get onto the more interesting facts about this boring middle aged writer, like how he once had rather too much to drink with some pals of Julian Lennon, held crocodiles in Egypt, sailed a tall ship across the Bay of Islands, walked with wolves, danced on a volcano and almost drove a 4x4 off a Greek mountain. Now all THAT would make a good story...

John Lovell

John, an established singer-songwriter, composer, actor and stage performer, is now looking to add writing to his list of accomplishments as he looks to further his contribution to the arts. Recently retired from a career in I.T. and with a keen interest in science, he views the horror genre as an ideal medium to express himself.

Printed in Poland
by Amazon Fulfillment
Poland Sp. z o.o., Wrocław